NINA BOURAOUI (Rennes, 1967) is a French novelist. Among other works, she is the author of *La Voyeuse interdite* (Prix du Livre Inter, 1991), *Mes mauvaises pensées* (Prix Renaudot, 2005), and more recently *Tous les hommes désirent naturellement savoir* (*All Men Want to Know*, trans. by Aneesa Abbas Higgins) and *Otages* (Prix Anaïs Nin, 2020).

ANEESA ABBAS HIGGINS is an award-winning translator who translates mostly literary fiction from French. Her translation of Nina Bouraoui's *All Men Want to Know* (2021) was the recipient of a PEN Translates Award and her translation of Elisa Shua Dusapin's *Winter in Sokcho* (2021) was the winner of the 2021 National Book Award for Translated Literature. Other authors she has translated include Tahar Ben Jelloun, Vénus Khoury-Ghata and Ali Zamir. Her work has also appeared in Words Without Borders and Asymptote. Before becoming a literary translator she taught French for many years in an international school in London.

HELEN VASSALLO is Associate Professor of French and Translation at the University of Exeter (UK). She translates Francophone women's writing, with a particular focus on North Africa and the Middle East. Helen is the founder of Translating Women, an activist research project that engages with publishers, translators and other stakeholders to work against intersectional gender bias in the translated literature sector of the UK publishing industry.

Nina Bouraoui

Satisfaction

TRANSLATED FROM THE FRENCH
BY ANEESA ABBAS HIGGINS

PRESS

First published in English in Great Britain in 2022 by
Héloïse Press Ltd
4 Pretoria Road
Canterbury CT1 1QL
www.heloisepress.com

First published under the original French language title: *Satisfaction*
© 2021 by Editions Jean-Claude Lattès

This translation © Aneesa Abbas Higgins 2022

Cover design by Laura Kloos
Copy-edited by Ella Skilbeck-Porter
Text design and typesetting by Tetragon, London
Printed and bound in Great Britain by CPI Group (UK) Ltd, Croydon, CR0 4YY

This book is supported by the Institut français (Royaume-Uni)
as part of the Burgess programme.

Here's To You
from SACCO E VANZETTI
Words by Joan Baez
Music by Ennio Morricone

ISBN 978-1-7397515-3-1

Contents

Introduction

Nina Bouraoui was born in Rennes, France, in 1967, but moved to Algeria at the age of two and spent most of her childhood in Algiers before settling in Paris as an adult. She is an acclaimed writer in France, with a literary career spanning over three decades: her first novel, *La Voyeuse interdite* (Gallimard, 1991), won the Prix du Livre Inter in 1991, and in 2005 she was awarded the prestigious Prix Renaudot for *Mes mauvaises pensées* (Stock, 2005), the third in a loose trilogy of her autofictional explorations of national and sexual identity.[1] In 2018 Bouraoui was awarded the highest decoration of the *Ordre des Arts et des Lettres*, in recognition of her contribution to literary heritage in France, and in 2020 she won the Prix Anaïs Nin for *Otages* (JC Lattès, 2020), which focused on social and gendered violence.

Born five years after the end of the Algerian War of Independence, Nina Bouraoui did not live through the trauma of the war, yet its traces are woven through much of her writing. Her literary work is marked by memories of violence and separation, by a sense of not belonging and by repressed trauma. These features are invariably linked to women's experience: to the fragility of being a woman in a culture where men are all-powerful, to the difficulty and loneliness of non-normative and forbidden desires, to the vulnerability that goes hand in hand with gendered and sexual difference. Bouraoui's early work is rooted in the newly independent Algeria of her childhood, and includes reflections on the victimisation she endured as a child because of the difference and divide that she represented as the daughter of a French mother and an Algerian father.

Nina Bouraoui's work has been translated into many languages, yet her recent novel *All Men Want to Know* (*Tous les hommes désirent naturellement savoir*, JC Lattès 2018) was the first of her works to be translated and published in the UK (in a translation by Aneesa Abbas Higgins for Penguin Books, 2021).[2] *All Men Want to Know* marked a shift in Bouraoui's writing: for the first time she began to offer an intimate and detailed account of both her sexual awakening and the difficulty of disentangling her desire for women from the violence of men. *All Men Want to Know* returned to a venue that featured prominently in the prize-winning *Mes mauvaises pensées*: the Parisian lesbian nightclub where a young Nina first felt that there was a place where she could be accepted.

In *Satisfaction* Nina Bouraoui continues this excavation of her past, but returns to the location, period and themes of her critically acclaimed coming-of-age novel, *Garçon manqué* (*Tomboy*). In this early novel, first published in 2000, Bouraoui wrote about a child called Nina Bouraoui, growing up in Algeria in the 1970s with a French mother and Algerian father, and coming to the realisation that she was attracted to women. *Tomboy* was written in short, clipped sentences, reflecting the fractured identity and experience of the narrator, and did not unfold chronologically. *Satisfaction* has an adult narrator and is written in longer, lyrical sentences: where Nina in *Tomboy* struggled with the impossibility of naming her experience, Madame Akli in *Satisfaction* becomes obsessed with immortalising hers in her notebooks of desire.

Though Nina Bouraoui's work is critically acclaimed and widely read throughout France and beyond, it has taken a long time for her writing to come to the attention of an English-language readership outside academic contexts. It is, sadly, not unusual that a contemporary woman writer with success both at home and abroad should be overlooked in the Anglophone world in this way. For an example of this we need look no further than Annie Ernaux, a literary icon in France, yet relatively unknown in the UK until Fitzcarraldo Editions began publishing her work in translation in 2018.[3] Like Ernaux, Bouraoui blurs the boundaries of fiction and autobiography and grounds her work within women's bodily experience and in relation to the socio-political contexts that have shaped her. There is a growing body of work recently translated from French that echoes this approach, and within which Bouraoui's work – and

Satisfaction in particular – is more broadly located: the literary sensation *All About Sarah* (2020) by Pauline Delabroy-Allard also explored shifting sexual desires in older women, while Négar Djavadi's award-winning *Disoriental* similarly deals with non-normative sexualities as well as situations of exile. Alice Zeniter's *The Art of Losing* delves, like much of Bouraoui's work, into the legacy of the Algerian War of Independence and its impact on those who did not live through it; meanwhile, the importance of photographs and images as snapshots of a decisive moment echoes *Selfies*, Sylvie Weil's collection of vignettes inspired by women's self-portraits, as well as *The Years*, Ernaux's collective autobiography. The diary-style writing and parasitic relationship between characters recalls *Self Portrait in Green* by Prix Goncourt winner Marie NDiaye, while the connection of characters to the cities and spaces they inhabit is echoed in Jakuta Alikavazovic's *Night as it Falls*.[4] That Bouraoui's work sits so well with such a range of titles (commissioned in translation by a variety of publishing houses) is testament to both its literary merit and its universal appeal. It also highlights the importance of making space for women's writing – particularly texts from other cultures that focus on marginalised experiences – in the Anglophone literary market, an endeavour that characterises the work of Héloïse Press.

Sensual, carnal and yearning, *Satisfaction* is the story of a woman who has lived the wrong life. Born in France, Michèle Akli has chosen to live in Algiers with her Algerian husband and is raising their adolescent son, Erwan. Yet she is painfully aware that she will never be accepted in Algeria and never be loved there; the life she has chosen thus becomes a form of exile. She is cut off from her past, from her roots and, ultimately, from herself, yet she cannot legitimately frame her experience within the context of exile, for this violent separation was not imposed on her but rather chosen when she married Brahim: mixed marriages are, Michèle explains, 'marriages of traitors' (p. 210). Brahim himself is a relatively unremarkable character, a wrong choice. Though he is depicted as a sweet and attentive husband, this is not enough for Michèle: she yearns for fulfilment of carnal desires that Brahim can no longer inspire in her. Her rejection of him borders on disgust: she dismisses their relationship as a mistake and cannot even retrieve companionship from the ashes of her initial passion. Indeed, she finds herself unable to tell Brahim of her terrifying and disempowering experiences as a woman in the streets of Algiers for fear of him turning on his own race, a form of externalised self-loathing born of the colonial history and of his marriage to a French woman. Like the marriage of Nina's parents in *Tomboy*, Brahim and Michèle's relationship comes to represent 'the failed history of our two countries' (p. 97) and the impossibility of union: they can never truly be joined because of the history that divides them and that has never been fully reconciled.

Madame Akli is, in many ways, reminiscent of Nina's mother in *Tomboy*: a French woman living in Algeria – with all of the social and political weight this label carries – whose existence there is precarious and never accepted. Yet this 'parallel' character in the early novel is little more than a spectre, barely visible and barely speaking. It is only in Bouraoui's more recent work that she has begun to write in detail about both her relationship with her mother and her mother's experience, and in *Satisfaction* she plunges deeper still into this past. Where Nina in *Tomboy* grew up in a post-Independence Algeria whose contours were sharply hewn, in *Satisfaction* Michèle Akli inhabits those years, filling out their edges as she claims them for herself and her generation, unfortunate heirs to a 'decade of fire' (p. 61). Throughout *Satisfaction*, Bouraoui thus returns to the spaces of her childhood and the themes of her early work, but with a more adult exploration of the desires and taboos that characterised those pieces.

If Madame Akli calls to mind Nina's mother in *Tomboy*, there are also echoes of Nina in Bruce, the young girl who befriends Erwan and whose grip on him threatens the bonds that tie him to his mother. Bruce has adopted a masculine self-presentation, taking her pseudonym from Bruce Lee; this stereotype of performative masculinity recalls Nina's attempts in *Tomboy* to walk like John Wayne, and to take on the persona of 'Ahmed' in order to reject the fragility and vulnerability that are irrevocably tied to female identity in this context. Bruce has 'changed her name in a bid to alter her fate' (p. 135), opting to incarnate masculine strength and power, yet we see this as a further violence inflicted on her, a 'murder' of her feminine self in order for a boy-child to be born in her place.

Just as in *Tomboy* where Nina was feared by her friend Amine's parents to be 'contagious', Bruce is seen as a danger, as a contaminant and as a rival, a threat to the bond Michèle shares with Erwan. With the revelation that Bruce's birth name is Amina, it is impossible not to see echoes in this character of both Amine and Nina from *Tomboy*. Yet in this more mature piece, roles are not black and white: rather, they are blurred, nuanced and rich in detail. The danger Bruce represents is not understood exclusively as one of sexuality, as this is not unequivocally imbricated with gender identity in the way it was in *Tomboy*. There is, nonetheless, still a 'contagion' associated with homosexuality, as we see in Michèle's explicitly voiced fear that she does not want her son to become homosexual and in her desire for him to be 'normal' – all the while despising herself for feeling this way. However, this fear is located within a more subtle exploration of the maternal role and the struggles of letting go. Michèle's love for her son is all-consuming: she becomes his cage, her womb still attached to him and not the other way round. Bruce comes to represent the enemy that Michèle must vanquish in her battle for her son's affections, a toxic influence from whom she must disentangle her beloved son. Erwan himself offers an interesting depth to the reflection on masculinity and femininity: he is portrayed as more defenceless than Bruce, described as physically fragile and emotionally vulnerable. Bouraoui thus plays with stereotypes of gender, softening the boundaries in a more delicate way than the intransigence of the starkly defined options available in her coming-of-age autofiction.

Yet just as Madame Akli is repulsed by Bruce, she is drawn to Bruce's mother, Catherine, the two women increasingly thrown together on extracurricular activities ostensibly focused on their inseparable adolescent children. Michèle becomes obsessed with Catherine, who comes to represent everything she herself longs to be. Michèle's sexual desires are bound up with her desire to be other than she is, but Catherine's feelings are significantly less intense. Nonetheless, Michèle's almost vampiric feelings towards Catherine are mirrored in the way that Catherine befriends her: she inhabits Michèle's experience, redefining all her cherished places and dispossessing Michèle of her familiar landscapes in ways that are both intoxicating and devastating. This connection of bodies and landscapes teases out themes that recur throughout *Satisfaction* (and indeed throughout Bouraoui's work more generally): the embodiment of the Algerian land and the vulnerability of women's bodies in public spaces. Madame Akli is at risk because of both her nationality and her gender; these two aspects of her identity come together in the way that she is venomously named a *'roumia'* (foreign woman) and pursued by whisperings about 'the sad French woman' (p. 55). Condemned to her role, Madame Akli becomes accustomed to hiding herself so that her face is not visible. The threat of male violence lurks everywhere she goes, as she is persecuted by shadows both real and imagined: these shadows taunt her, leaving her feeling that she is always observed and always exposed.

As in much of Bouraoui's work, both the Algerian landscape and the legacy of the Algerian War of Independence weigh heavily on the lives of the protagonists. The sinister implications of this are manifest in Michèle's recognition that she cannot escape the weight of 'Algerian soil on French women's shoulders' (p. 67). This soil is variously storm-drenched, soaked in blood or gouged up by intruders, yet it is also a refuge for Michèle: she tills her garden, tries to coax into life plants which are later crushed with her emotional disappointments, and likens herself to a plant growing in stony ground. She is uprooted from her homeland, her memories of France amounting to nothing more than a 'mausoleum' (p. 102), and instead she attempts to negotiate a new life in a place where she lives with the constant possibility of being murdered. As elsewhere in Bouraoui's œuvre, the sea that divides the two countries represents both a place of freedom, unfettered from the restrictions of the landscape, and a danger, a force that could drag Michèle under and consume her.

Another recognisable theme from elsewhere in Bouraoui's work is illness: this is invariably depicted as something socially cast onto the 'ill' person (usually a woman), or born out of the impossibility of self-expression. In *Satisfaction* Madame Akli describes fear and desire as illnesses, and these interwoven maladies crash in on her and exacerbate her isolation, driving her to spend her days drinking, to the point where she becomes a recluse and the family closes in on itself. As she sinks deeper into this fever-ish isolation she fears that she is going mad, and acknowledges that not only are fear and desire forms of illness, but that sadness is too. These perceived illnesses are more externalised in *Satisfaction* than in Bouraoui's earlier works,

drawing explicit links between the role cast on the protag-
onist in the 'visible' Algeria and her descent into a kind of
madness because of the dangers beneath the surface.

This alienation is given substance through writing:
Madame Akli's notebooks, which are the metatext of
Satisfaction, are where all of her fears and desires take shape.
These 'notebooks of shame' (p. 204) have a hallucinatory
quality, but also a rage that reflects the violence of the context. In *Satisfaction* we witness a writer at the height of her
storytelling career and a translator who breathes new life
into an extraordinary work: sensitive to the savage beauty
and quiet obsessions, the looming shadows and the oppressive heat, Aneesa Abbas Higgins recasts this story for an
English-language readership, teasing out the rugged contours of the landscape, the fragrance of jasmine, the heavy
scent of the vegetation and the smells of Catherine's body,
the instincts, dreams and desires that fill Madame Akli's life,
the weight of history and the brooding silence that hangs
over the narrative. The oppressive heat of Algiers comes to
life in Abbas Higgins' translation as a panorama of 'jagged
outlines', a landscape of fragments riddled with barbed wire
and populated by shadows.

Yet if Madame Akli's books are where all her shame is
contained, this externalisation offers her a possible redemp-
tion: if silence imprisons her in shame, words can purge
it, repair the damage 'like a needle and thread mending torn fabric' (p. 53). Words are, then, both a defence
and an attack in this novel of desire and desolation: the
notebook a weapon and words themselves 'a round of

ammunition' (p. 55). With her words Michèle carves out her identity and experience, expresses all that is repressed and connects herself to the world around her. This is manifest in the importance of music and lyrics, a feature that those already acquainted with Bouraoui's work will recognise from elsewhere in her œuvre (in particular, it is revealed towards the end of Michèle's story where the title of the book comes from). Michèle Akli's notebooks are variously her shame, her refuge and her memory: in them she liberates herself from the judgement of others but exposes herself to her own. Her voice is haunting, her story compelling: *Satisfaction* is a savage expression of longing, a determined facing-down of shame, a painful reflection on women's vulnerability and a remarkable exploration of the multiple ways in which love and desire can inhibit and inhabit us.

Helen Vassallo, July 2022

NOTES

1 The first two books in the 'trilogy' are *Garçon manqué* (Stock, 2000) and *Poupée Bella* (Stock, 2004).

2 Both *Forbidden Vision* and *Tomboy* have previously been published in English translation in the US. *Forbidden Vision*, translated by Melissa Marcus (Station Hill Press, 1995); *Tomboy*, translated by Marjorie Attignol Salvodon and Jehanne-Marie Gavarini (University of Nebraska Press, 2007).

3 To date Fitzcarraldo has published eight of Ernaux's works, all translated by either Alison L. Strayer or Tanya Leslie. In October 2022 Ernaux became the 17th woman laureate of the Nobel Prize in Literature, an international recognition that is likely to bring increased attention to her work.

4   Pauline Delabroy-Allard, *All About Sarah*, translated by Adriana Hunter
    (Penguin, 2020); Négar Djavadi, *Disoriental*, translated by Tina Kover
    (Europa Editions, 2018); Alice Zeniter, *The Art of Losing*, translated by
    Frank Wynne (Pan Macmillan, 2021), Sylvie Weil, *Selfies*, translated by
    Ros Schwartz (Les Fugitives, 2019); Annie Ernaux, *The Years*, translated
    by Alison L. Strayer (Fitzcarraldo Editions, 2018); Marie NDiaye, *Self
    Portrait in Green*, translated by Jordan Stump (Influx Press, 2021); Jakuta
    Alikavazovic, *Night as it Falls*, translated by Jeffrey Zuckerman (Faber &
    Faber, 2021).

MADAME AKLI'S SEVEN NOTEBOOKS

(Algiers, 1977–1978)

I

The air is so warm, so dense, you can almost see it in the Polaroid snapshots I take. A halo surrounds the bodies of the people I photograph: Erwan, my son, his fawn-like slenderness yet to be supplanted by masculine strength, his curls, his dark eyes, his face, in which I see nothing of myself, reflecting his father Brahim's features. They're both looking off to the right, avoiding the camera lens, evading me, absorbed by something in the distance: Erwan, gazing out to sea while I stand back on the beach, Brahim, eyes fixed on the street as I snap him from our garden.

They have left me behind to come together in that imaginary zone reserved for men.

The geography of my garden echoes the atlases of my childhood. Set between the maps of the oceans were posters I collected of exotic gardens. In my dreams I was elsewhere, somewhere away from France, land of my birth, where I grew up but where I shall not grow old.

I came to Algeria in 1962, after Independence, newly wedded to Brahim and following in his wake. I'm thirty-eight now. Algeria has become my country, the landscape of my twenties and thirties. One day it will be my tomb.

I have led the wrong life. I wish this weren't true, but I'm committing it to paper now, distancing myself from it by putting words on a page. Words can make us believe in the illusion that language has the power to heal, or at least to transform reality and provide consolation for our defeats. I'm waiting for something, an event, but I know nothing about it. In truth, I should say that I'm waiting for someone.

I love Brahim, but not with the passion of the first days, when love consumes everything, internally and externally, invading the space we move through, confounding sound and silence, making routine festive, transforming suffering into fulfilment. I no longer feel the wholeness of our union. The shame I feel at writing these words is the reason for this journal. Shame has a place, here, and from now on, this is where it must stay.

Birds of paradise, my favourite flowers. Through the sheer curtains of our bedroom window they look like children bowing their heads in prayer, or perhaps in anticipation of punishment. Beyond them are succulents and palm trees, the thread-like bark of their resinous trunks transformed into creepers, then jasmine, wisteria and mimosa, their flowery clusters like flesh in my hands. Nature's beauty is full of sadness, impossible to admire it without weeping, to ascend to its heights without falling. They say there is still blood in the soil here, blood that can only be purged by another revolution. I believe that History repeats itself, I believe in the eternal return of human folly.

I have an ominous feeling that something is going to happen, I don't know if it will come from the outside or if I'm going to invent it, generate it, draw it out from within me to contaminate those around me. The scenes and tableaux I imagine are harbingers of tragic events. At night, I have a vision of three bodies hanging from the branches of the oak tree. I fear for my son, I no longer fear for Brahim. My passion has been transferred.

My desire remains because it's not tied to our relationship. It's directed towards Brahim's body, as it could be towards any other body, I need only to be relieved of it. My desire goes beyond me, it governs me and leaves me melancholic when its fulfilment proves disappointing.

A smell of burning rises from Algiers to Hydra, our neighbourhood. Ash covers the bonnets of cars. Fire rains down from the sky. The mountain is ablaze, a red snake coils over the peaks of Chréa; a single shard of glass is enough to ignite the trees, the mosses, the ferns. The smell of crude oil, from the tankers that transport it to Europe, mingles with the flames. I am a dot on the African continent, alone with my family, bodies dissociated from the landscape that contains and threatens them.

As the French were leaving Algeria by sea after the war, I arrived by air in a Caravelle. I was to pay the price for my arrogance and treachery. I melted into the crowd at first, but our destinies were to diverge, despite the land we shared. I was discovering that land while my countrymen were leaving, taking none of it with them, nothing that could be transplanted to adapt and grow beneath other skies. For a sky is unique, it cannot be replaced. To love a sky is to love a landscape, a forest, a stream, a favourite rock, a platform from which to dive and test oneself against all of creation.

But those who left were Algerian, not French, unrecognised by any state. I wasn't interested in their suffering, it meant nothing to me. Politics is a source of division. I was caught up in a cause I did not understand, I didn't realise that freedom is not a natural state, that if it's stolen, it must be relearnt. I clung to Brahim, stayed close to his family, his people. I embraced them as I embrace my man, pressing my lips to his belly in search of solace when I feel orphaned from my past. Skin is the refuge of those who have no ties.

Those 'French' people from Algeria are prisoners of nostalgia. Memory is cruel, we call on it to rekindle burnt-out fires, but with the years, it fades, leading us down phantom paths, like beggars searching for traces of our past, towards houses that never existed. Memory is their punishment, mine lay in my beginning. Violence endures, its medusa-like tentacles live on. I have become a second-generation coloniser. I shall not be loved here.

While the fires burn, I stay home with Erwan. The road to the beach is lined with reeds. As soon as the storms are over and the marshland dries out again, I fear being trapped by the flames, unable to escape. We must wait. The fires will die down when there is nothing left to consume, when stone proves stronger than the flames.

Brahim leaves early for his paper factory a few kilometres outside Algiers, a family legacy he has sworn to keep in memory of his parents. I hear the sound of his car starting up, the door slamming and I wonder what would become of us if he didn't come back. Would I have the courage to leave, to start a new life? I doubt it. Time binds us to our home.

The heat has stalled the passage of time, seconds become minutes, minutes turn to hours. Every gesture is burdensome, fragmented into a million invisible movements. Nothing engages Erwan, not cards, nor dice, not even his race-car track, he says he's tired of it, he's too old for it, he's ten now. I give him a job to do, descaling and flouring the red mullet, a job he likes, but he refuses to do it. He can't stand the smell of blood, he says. We leave the fish on ice.

We move around the house in search of treasure, seeking out cool and shade. I lock onto my notebook, Erwan walks through the living room to his bedroom, comes back out again, goes out to the garage looking for tools to repair a fan I'd stored with all the things I can't throw out: birthday cards, letters from my parents, from my brother, bills, child-ish drawings from Erwan's first years at school, a record player, flotsam of a life begun, objects I hang onto to pre-serve the lives of those I love, to keep alive my son's child-hood and the hope that Brahim and I will dance together again as we did at the height of our passion.

When the sun is high in the sky, the garden becomes a hot-house that threatens to engulf us, devour our flesh, while the most delicate of blooms seem to flourish in the intense heat: lilac and privet, plants without names, plants that sting and grate, weeds, golden buds, velvet shoots, all growing in profusion.

Erwan in blue shorts, bare-chested. Watching him grow, I discover a new muscle every day and imagine him as the young man he will become. His strength is concentrated in his shoulders and torso, his thighs slender by contrast, his arms skinny.

His body grows unevenly, in irregular spurts, beginning with the parts where power and desire originate. I am moved by my son's beauty, I can see his manhood in waiting, passed down to him by Brahim and wrapped in fragility, the legacy of my femininity – my repressed femininity. But femininity should not be confused with fragility. They are not the same.

We spray each other with the hose, dump buckets of water on each other's heads, throw water bombs. We cling to one another, dripping wet, like survivors of a disaster, fortunate escapees handed the curse of bearing witness to the destruction of houses, buildings, the entire city.

Brahim is no longer either husband or father, he is out at work, busy in his factory, leaving us no choice but to experience our first Algerian summer.

We usually leave Algiers in the summer holidays; we all go to Paris to see my brother, then I take Erwan to my parents' by the sea in Brest and rejoin Brahim in a city of our choosing in Europe; before long, I start missing my son, I become obsessed with Algeria again as if the two were bound together, essential elements of my well-being. Last summer, while we were in Vienna, the city began to close in on me. I became stone and walls, a piece of the sky and the night, imprisoned in the buildings and monuments, the dark waters of the Danube, the countryside, the weeping willows we lay beneath, avoiding one another's touch, not embracing. We had become strangers.

Our summer revolves around our house and the beaches of nearby Staoueli. Brahim would be able to get there quickly if anything were to happen. We live with this possibility.

I was not forced to flee my country, I wasn't persecuted. I am exiled in my very soul. I'm on the outside of something that's floated away, ceased to exist, evaporated. But to me it is still palpable, a circle that holds my memories and the dreams of my youth. My kind of exile, from the self, if such a thing exists, would be better described as 'the abandonment of hope'.

The sky is heavy with flames that threaten to descend upon the villages and contaminate the whole country. It will be the oueds, the hills, the ravine and the sea that will protect us, not our position overlooking the port and the beach resorts that have fallen into disuse, abandoned by the colonisers, with the infrastructure still intact. Hatred of the past means that we have let time do its work of destruction.

From the roof, a view of the gardens, the houses of the neighbours whom I greet for the sake of politeness. I haven't managed to form any friendships since we've been living in this neighbourhood. The Algerian families keep to themselves. Mixed couples are looked down upon, the Algerian husbands suspected of spying, of being traitors, their Western wives seen as women of ill-repute, mere sex objects according to local legend. The French families stationed here for a limited time don't mix with anyone else. They act as if they are living in an outpost of France and leave without ever exploring the city. Decolonisation is like the receding of flood waters, every twist and turn must be followed in sequence like a river draining from the land it has ravaged. The few friends we do have were originally Brahim's.

Beyond the fig and medlar trees, the smallest trees in our garden, we can see the palm groves of Bou Saada. We feel like kings perched here above the rooftops, but we are ruled by the harshness of the climate. When Brahim comes home, I have to get used to him again, his voice, his skin, I lose familiarity with them quickly. Erwan rushes to greet his father, throws his arms around his waist, takes hold of his hands, his shoulders, sparking in me a feeling of jealousy and doubt. I'm afraid that his days with me must seem so dull. Algiers is no place for a child.

Brahim's hands on my hips, his shirt damp with sweat, his beard against my skin, his thick hair, his aquiline nose: the physical reality of being married to a foreigner. I swell with pride, as if I were confronting danger – a racist notion. Does he see me as the French woman he tore away from her family? A trophy? Or does love obliterate geographical boundaries, ambitions, the desire for revenge? Does it exist simply because it must, because it is etched into the destiny of the lovers?

Night reveals the contours of a country that appeals to me more than the realm of daylight. Alcohol drags me from my anxiety. From the very first glass, a lake forms inside me, an oasis of calm, surrounded by a forest of maple trees, like a lake in Canada. It subsumes me, outgrows me, outstrips the heat, the city of Algiers, dwarfs everything. My level of intoxication is under my control, it's light, I know it well, I float on its surface, the best part. With delicate gestures I build desire, a castle in the sand that will be engulfed by the first wave. When the alcohol wears off, I'll go back to my discomfort, my cracks and fissures.

In our kisses, the taste of watermelon, honeydew melon, fruits of the garden. Our lips, tongues, mouths, lush with sugar.

Brahim sits on the steps of the terrace, Erwin lights the lanterns. I don't know if Brahim is putting on an act, if it's me he's looking at as I pick flowers for a bouquet, whether he's realised that alcohol was bringing me closer to him or if, with his glass of whisky, he's imagining a wider existence for himself, with a happier wife. I berate myself for no longer being as I used to be before; but before what? Haven't I always been haunted by a melancholy that no country, no voyage, no flight could appease or cure? The melancholy that led me to Algeria, where the past and present exist side by side, where Roman remains are scattered here and there, ruins that contain human destinies. The earth is waiting for them, it will reclaim them.

We are afraid the wind from the south will whip up the flames, scattering embers at the foot of the mountain, ravaging remote villages as the war did – hamlets laid waste to by soldiers looking for partisans. This is nature as tragedy, bent on destruction. The fires are one with my desire, but the object of that desire is not Brahim's body, it is another body, working through his. Brahim is the conduit for another, his double. I'm laying the groundwork for my feelings, rehearsing them, as if for a play. I'm acting love before living it, inhabiting it. Love is a space that I've left, that I must find again. I come into its orbit again with Erwan, but maternal love is no replacement for carnal love. They're two distinct, parallel forms of love.

The night is lit from within by the flames. Erwan runs around the garden singing 'Upside down', the refrain from the record on the turntable, summing up my state of mind, even though the song is about attraction, arousal and the mess it creates. I veer from high to low, never stopping to dig for the roots of the things that trouble me.

Brahim, his shoulders, his way of watching his son, of smoking his cigarette, the back of his neck, his powerful thighs, his stone-coloured trousers, his bare feet in his moccasins, his elegance, the patience of a man who reproaches me for nothing, asks for so little.

Squeezing lemons and oranges, crushing them as I crush my frustration. The years are passing, I watch them slip by. I play my part as mother, wife. I drift through the seasons, immobile, while birds migrate to the south of the continent. I wish I could work, I'm a trained teacher, but I refuse to work at Erwan's school and put pressure on my son, I don't want to exert authority over him as a teacher, my authority is that of a mother. Power would be passed back and forth between school and home, saturation point would be reached. And I'm afraid of shaming Erwan.

I can write in this notebook that I don't like myself. I'm not talking about beauty, I don't think I'm ugly, there's no such thing as ugliness, there is always something to take from a face, a body. I'm proud of my body, my slender, willowy frame. When I say 'I don't like myself', what I mean is that I don't know myself. My femininity eludes me, even though I'm sexually active, I've given birth, which women say is a revelation. I felt nothing like that, only the sensation of being a body-machine delivering itself of a burden. It didn't stop me from loving my son; my love for him is jealous, exclusive, I have suffered for him, he is my due, he belongs to me.

My desire is a force. Men are obsessed with relief. I give Brahim pleasure, my orgasm is a response to his, not the reverse.

When I look at myself in the mirror, I see the potential for my feminine self; it wouldn't take much, a touch of make-up, a change of hairstyle, some new clothes and there it would be. Because of the men in the street, I dress discreetly – my loose shirts, trousers, long skirts don't arouse any desire. When Brahim comes back from his travels I make an effort for his sake. I greet him, ready, as if I've been waiting for him, missing him, which happens less and less often. When I'm alone with Erwan I feel a calmness. I put on a show when we invite friends, Brahim's work colleagues, I slip into an unfamiliar skin that's ready and waiting to move centre stage. It takes time to learn who one is, to get to know oneself. I grew up with a brother, I'm still growing up, with a son, a husband, in Algiers, the city of men. What I lack is a woman beside me.

Brahim declares his love for what he calls my subtle beauty, he says he can sense its glow when his lips brush my cheek, when his body enfolds mine; my mind turns elsewhere, using his flesh to lead me to a different tableau, other games. My guilt, even though I remain faithful. Is it possible to love when love is absent? I try to frame our sensuality, our bedroom is as narrow as the chambers of my heart, I have so much yet to find out, so much to give.

What would Brahim think if he read my journal? He'd be saddened, I expect, to learn that I'm suffering here in this country we used to call the Starred Eldorado. My need for words would not surprise him: 'Women need to tell themselves stories.' He wouldn't recognise himself in its pages. If only it was all an invention.

On the steps of our terrace, pressed up against Brahim, his arm around my shoulders, two people; I'm conscious of my own oneness, my imagination carries me beyond the garden, out into the street, away from the town and the port, up towards the hills. I climb, eyes closed, through a hail of ash. I reach the top and there it is, the massive, modern structure, its curved lines so different from the standard residential blocks of little white houses with their lemon trees and orange trees, wisteria and bougainvillea spilling over the walls, tongues of mauve, pink and red.

The Shell building keeps nature at bay, at a distance from its concrete piers, its balconies, its two façades, one of them pierced by lookout holes. It slices through the sky, every aspect of it designed to rule over us. Like a magnet, it draws me in. Only a mad person would want to inhabit this building, to make it their home.

Wine, a feeling of lightness, Brahim's breath, Erwan disappears into the garden; seated beneath the palm tree, he becomes part of the décor, a plant, his flesh grafted to the branches and the earth. He watches us; through my son's gaze, I am, I exist, my blood pulses with the sap of the succulents that sink their roots into the earth, their thirst slaked by water deep in the clay.

Crushing strawberries, raspberries, arranging them in bowls with ice cubes, one hour is enough to frost them. Erwan is excited by the night that wraps itself around us. Our son's happy childhood bestows happiness on us vicariously.

The sound of police sirens rising from the centre of Algiers brings back visions of tortured flesh, of throats, bellies, chests cut open with knives, faces gashed, burnt with acid, women punished, disfigured. I imagine fights, brawls in the narrow streets of the Casbah, visions of butchers' cleavers, barbers' razors, daggers with handles encrusted with gold, rubies, diamonds, weapons from the tales of the orient in the picture books I peruse with Erwan, as if violence itself were the stuff of stories.

Alcohol has the effect of creating different layers in my mind.

One layer for my son running from his bedroom to the garden, making me think seriously about his future: should I send him to France when he is old enough to go to university? Which nationality should he choose for his military service? What kind of future can he expect here? And how will I live without him one day? Erwan, my beloved.

A layer for Brahim, for desire, his hands, his torso. How to tell him of my sadness without hurting him?

A layer for France, my lost country, feeling in my blood that I am becoming a citizen of Algeria, absorbed by the city.

A layer of fear, not a fear of men, nor of nature, the government or the memory of history, but of myself, a fear of losing my way.

Brahim tells me that there's a vacancy for a librarian coming up at the French lycée. After the new cultural attaché arrives, he'll put in a word for me, if I want. I say yes, but there's no hurry, I don't mind waiting. Brahim sells paper to the school: white paper, carbon paper, fine 'technical' paper infused with a liquid that gives black ink a purple tinge. The French lycée is a place of refuge: Moorish architecture, palm trees, banana trees, underground passages leading to the docks of Algiers, escape routes through the earth's underground galleries. I imagine myself surrounded by books, fleeing.

Our evenings always end the same way, Erwan falls asleep in my lap, Brahim gathers him in his arms and carries him to his bedroom, puts him to bed, kisses him, turns on his nightlight, leaves the door ajar, goes back to check on him once, twice, three times and then opens another bottle of wine. I stay outside in the garden. I'm no longer looking up at the sky, the heavens are looking down on me, knowing that I'm pretending. The palm trees bend, as if guided by a force set in motion outside our house, beyond our control; a divine order, obeyed by the elements, and by us.

Our voices intertwine, not responding to each other, we each have our own story to tell, we don't realise they won't intersect, that we won't be included in each other's account of the day nor in each other's account of our doubts and reflections. We are two runners, our backs turned, each on a different path.

Brahim's naked body. I close my eyes. I invent a *him* and a *her*. I imagine a woman in Brahim's place. I feel no desire for women, no sense of arousal. This thought divides me in two, I catch a glimpse of myself in the image I create, I recognise my outline, but not my face. The wine goes to my head, I'm distracted. Pleasure comes and fades away. None of it remains, only the awareness of the garden beyond the sheer curtains on the bedroom window, plants growing, jostling for space. On the bedside table, a grey pebble enclosed in a white circle, a stone replicating itself, changing colour, being reborn. I dream of becoming another person, of creating an other from myself.

This morning, as I drove with Erwan to the beach, there was a man following us. I don't know if he was waiting for us outside our house or if he crossed our path by chance; I didn't see anything out of the ordinary when I drove out of the garage but I'm not sure, we're always so wrapped up in our routines, our gestures, we don't pay attention to our surroundings, or we don't look hard enough, we don't see what's changed. I noticed him once we were on the dual carriageway. I didn't mention it to Erwan.

Earlier, at the boulangerie in Place d'Hydra, we bought some Cocas, turnovers filled with tomatoes, courgettes and onions. Then we headed downhill towards the sea. The fire on the mountain had died down.

He's driving a small car, a battered white Renault 8. He stares at us as he overtakes us and cuts in front, forcing me to brake. Then he slows down, lets me pass him.

I lower the windows, it's so hot. Erwan is sitting in a strange position behind me, on the edge of his seat, glued to the back of mine, his arm around my neck. He seems worried, afraid I might detach myself from him, like a capsule separating from the rest of the rocket as it is hurtled into space.

We turn off the main road onto the grassy track that leads to the beach and the man disappears from view.

The road narrows. I roll up the windows to avoid being scratched by the reeds and bushes.

The smell of salt marshes, seaweed, scorched earth, ash and mud after the fires, the whistling sound of the wind in the reeds that surround the bushy hideaway.

I pull up in the Zeralda beach car park. We unload the car. Erwan takes the parasol, the ball, the beach towels, I'm in charge of the cooler and the things we bought at the shops in Hydra.

Heat rises from the tarmac underfoot, a smell of straw, like a henhouse.

Erwan kicks off his sandals, drops everything, peels off his clothes, runs towards the water and dives in. I gather up his clothes, set up the beach umbrella, spread out the beach towels, anchoring them with rocks, the wind is picking up.

My eyes are gritty with sand, I don't recognise the man at first, the one who followed us. He's standing above the beach. A shadow, blocking out the sun.

Erwan vanishes beneath the waves, comes back up again, a creature from the depths, happy, aware of my admiring gaze. My son is a good swimmer, fearless in the water, his slenderness becomes a force that makes him bold, agile.

A group of Algerian women have made a shelter out of four sticks and a blanket. Huddled together, their laughter mingles with the sound of the waves as they rise, swell and break.

Aunts, sisters, mothers, they talk with one hand over their mouth to mask the venom of their words, probably talking about the *roumia*, the foreign woman, me, and the wretched spectacle I make to them, the *mesquina*, the woman alone with her child.

The sea is rough, I watch Erwan closely, sensing a presence behind me. Something might be about to happen, I force myself not to turn around. I sit with my knees pressed to my chest, ready to leap up and save my son from the waves.

The Algerian women have stopped looking at me. I wish Brahim were here. I feel thrown off course by the violence of the waves and the swirling sands, powerless against enemies of my own invention.

I'm wearing a black one-piece swimsuit, sunglasses that obscure my features, my skin dotted with freckles. I'm not like the women here, I'm different.

Erwan emerges from the water, runs towards me, his gaze fixed on something far behind me, as if pulled by an invisible hand, a leash tethered to a tree. He draws level with me and stops, fists clenched, tired out by the waves. Still staring into the distance, he asks me where sand comes from. I say something about erosion, dust, particles, trying not to show my concern. The man comes and sits down near us.

Hundreds of sea anemones lie scattered on the beach, thrown up onto the sand by the waves. As the day goes on the smell rising from the rotting corpses adds to the sickly stench in the car park. The Algerian women have been driven away by the wind, all signs of the sticks they used to anchor their make-shift tent will soon be gone, obliterated, succumbing like our flesh to the elements. The rollers churn up gravel – brown, white, grey, transparent – crystals of precious stone shattered on another continent. The sea claims everything, gemstones, sea anemones, it will claim our bodies too if this man is intending to kill us.

He lies back, propped up on his elbows, ankles crossed. Flannel trousers, short-sleeved white shirt, leather shoes, I recognise the uniform worn by government employees. He stands up, I draw closer to Erwan who hasn't sensed my fear and seems oblivious to the man's performance, maybe I'm imagining it all – the man has taken off his shoes and socks and is walking down to the shoreline. He stands facing the water, the waves as high as the wall that divides our garden from the street. He turns around and looks at us, his gaze persistent, haughty. A hunter confronting his prey, preparing to avenge a previous humiliation. He knows I've understood; he's issuing a challenge, just as he did on the road. Shoes in hand, trousers rolled up to the knee, he has us directly in his sights. I can't leave the beach, he'd catch up with us, force us into the marshes.

A circle of light dances on the sand. I think back to the night of the fires, to Brahim. Sorrow pours from me like water, I feel it flowing from my flesh. Nature has made a pact with my sadness, injecting me with melancholy and reclaiming it when I am overwhelmed by the vertigo it induces. Freed from my body, my sadness meets the earth, the sea, before coming back to my skin.

The circle of light settles on Erwan's right leg, then his left, I can't see where the reflections are coming from. It lands on my thigh, my stomach, struggling to settle on its target, deflected by the wind or by the lack of skill of whoever is controlling it remotely, sending it towards us: a warning sign.

The man advances, the circle emanates from his watch face, I don't know if he's noticed, if he's doing it intentionally, if the flashes of light are aimed at me, against me, heightening the dramatic tension of the scene and its players: the driver, the storm-swept beach, the tumultuous sea, Erwan, who hasn't grasped the seriousness of what is possibly unfolding. I'm cowardly enough to think that my child will protect me, will force the man to walk on by. The man smiles at Erwan and addresses me: *la takhfou*, he says, 'Don't be afraid.' On his badge, clipped to his shirt pocket, his name and surname written in Arabic. I don't recognise the logo of the company he works for, but I can see his face on the photo, a face I promise myself I won't forget, as if this man had actually beaten me, injured me. He moves away, climbs the dune that divides the car park from the beach, no longer looking at us. I hear his car starting up. I pick up our things, the beach is blighted, we have to leave.

Erwan asleep, knocked out by the force of the waves, the blasting wind and swirling sand. The road through the reeds seems wider, as if space has been stretched by the heat. I imagine the man lurking in the reeds, setting a trap for us, in his hand the knife he's used to cut his way through the marshy undergrowth.

La takhfou: a prophetic message. Foretelling my future, telling me to look into the darker corners of my mind.

The Zeralda street hawker waits by the side of the road for customers. Beside him, sheltered from the wind, a child sells caged sparrows. Poverty, among country folk and city dwellers alike; Algeria has passed from one set of hands to another, like a pack of cards. Material wretchedness mirrored in nature's melancholy, the trees, flowers and light weeping for men abandoned to their fate.

I wonder where the people who flock to leave the central port area go. Is there a place that can absorb them and stem the flow of people from the centre to the outlying districts? The sea is not a pleasure zone here, it is where people go to embark, to head out to sea and make for the coast of Spain. People say there will be another war, a second war that the military are secretly preparing. This country is made up of two worlds, one visible, the other unseen, a clandestine territory under construction, waiting to emerge and destroy.

The Beatles' 'Yellow Submarine' on the cassette player in the car. Erwan is wide awake, embracing the happiness it radiates. We sing at the tops of our voices, together inside our yellow submarine.

I often think about what will remain, what Erwan will retain of me, of his childhood. I wish I could capture his feelings with my camera, reveal them, engrave these moments on film. I'm afraid that love will fade along with memories; I want to preserve the scent of jasmine as we approach our house, the smell of a well-ordered household – despite the chaos in my heart – against the backdrop of tumultuous seas and man-made carnage, violence real or imagined. I want to shield our son from the events of the 1970s, from the march of Algeria's history towards chaos.

Pomegranate seeds and fresh almonds.
    The jagged outline of the rocks.
    The marshes with their animal smell.
    The man, the stranger, the enemy.
    Strains of chaabi music drifting out from a house.
    The click of the garden gate when Brahim comes home.
    The changing colour of Polaroid paper as it develops.
    The muezzin's voice and the call to prayer.
    The click-click of the Super 8 camera.
    The breeze in the curtains.
    Bouquets of thyme and coriander, zaatar and *kazbira*.
    My mind seizes upon fragments of the real world and absorbs them into my unconscious, I could stretch the list out to infinity. I am riddled with blows from the space

around me, from sounds and objects. Everything makes an impression. My mind spins, splinters of colour, turning like a kaleidoscope, changing direction under my command. I dream of a pure white light that reveals a landscape with no footprints, no signs of human presence.

I tend my plants, the shoots and seedlings, with my bare hands; I have faith in the magnetism of the earth, the power of the sky, I marvel at it in the early morning light, surrender to it at nightfall.

The sun has wrought changes in my skin, multiplying and darkening my freckles, skin washed by sea, wind and sand, by the presence of the man who followed us, spied on us. I resent him for instilling fear in me on the road through the reeds, the road that cuts through the heart of the marshes all the way to the gates of Algiers. I see him on every street corner, the city has taken on his features.

Brahim has brought back a plant from the desert, alfa, used for making paper. The alfa is dry, sharp-edged, like the notes I write this evening, sitting on the steps of the terrace dressed in my flesh-coloured see-through dress, a glass of wine beside me, trying to pin down life as it passes. I want to gather up all the details of our life and preserve them in my notebooks; that way we won't die.

Erwan plays with a feather he bought at the beginning of the summer by the side of the road to Koléa. He runs around the garden waving it like a spear, attacking shadows and clouds. My son's shoulder blades, wings that propel him forward as he runs. August is fading, its torpor lingers.

I plant the alfa beneath the palm tree, hoping to see it grow into a tree; every one of its flowers would be a souvenir of the three of us.

Algiers, city of sorrows.

I remember being struck by the beauty of the Palestro region shortly after Independence: the fields, the gigantic rock formations, the carpets of buttercups and asphodels, the ranks of daffodils and daisies, yellow flowers lit up by the sun, the terrifying cries of the monkeys, witnesses to slaughter. I was moved by the powerlessness of animals denied language, unable to tell their tale.

I say nothing to Brahim of the man who followed us, I'm afraid of how he might react, what he might say. He hates his own people sometimes, he feels he can no longer identify with those he once considered to be his brothers, he insults them, makes racist comments, slurs he was subjected to himself in the days of French Algeria. I see it as an inner loathing, a hatred of self projected onto others, a way of lightening his load to avoid the destruction of everything he has built with his son and me.

Lying on our stomachs, our bodies tense, taut, damp, our muscles swollen from effort, from desire, from the pressure of limbs seeking to intertwine, to break apart, from the confusion of breath, hair, skin, flesh. We could be locked in combat, one of us must cede ground, the conflict cannot be sustained, it is a fight to the death. I think of the praying mantis assassinating her chosen mate, of dogs fighting with bared teeth, tearing into necks, flanks, the back of the neck. Our bedroom battle is a striving for ecstasy, a plea for the orgasm that will deliver us from the heat, from ennui, from the failure of words.

Our kisses, devoid of tenderness, are substitutes for words. I can't say 'I've stopped loving you' to Brahim, any more than I could leave him; leave with my son, abandon his father here in this tragic country and learn how to live in another city with other men and other women. I'm condemned to stay, a sentence imposed on myself for lack of courage and imagination. I wouldn't know where to go.

The walls of the neighbouring houses have pieces of glass along the top to deter burglars. The area is patrolled by militia. It's said that men, five of them, like the *hamsa,* five fingers of the hand, come into the houses to spy, search. I don't know if the rumour is to be believed, but I do know that glowing embers are the first signs of fire.

The storm has drenched the soil, I hear the rustling of flowers as they open, gorged with rainwater, the cry of birds excited by night-time lightning. Insects, larvae, crawling, swarming, I imagine their secret language, the bond they share, their power. The earth is alive, overflowing, growing, coming back to life, nourished by its own shoots, peelings, debris. It smells, stinks, ravishes, intoxicates. It maddens, enslaves. The earth will devour my skin, my organs, my remains. It is indifferent, unregimented, free. It will survive the violence we do to it. It sings, makes gestures, opens and closes, flows with sap, resin. It dazzles with photosynthesis, transforms itself, comes back lustrous and renewed. The earth rejoices while I dwell on thoughts of summer's death.

I take Erwan up to the Paradou district to see the Thomson's gazelle. It's been there for several months now. Erwan flattens himself against the fence, the animal moves away, bows its head. I take a picture of my son, arms folded across his chest. He's wearing a red-striped T-shirt, white shorts, espadrilles. He gazes at me defiantly, like the man at the beach. In the frame, two creatures held captive: the gazelle in its enclosure, my son penned in by his mother. I am his cage. Erwan's face appears on the paper, Brahim's features no longer apparent. A ghostly shadow emerges instead, gradually saturating the image, the face of my fear.

II

The first day of the school year. Brahim is taking our son to the Petit Hydra school. Erwan waves without turning to look at me. I stand barefoot on the steps in my nightgown, watching them as they drive off. The car disappears from sight as they round the bend and vanish into the city. Alone again in the labyrinthine web of the house, my isolation no longer masked by the holidays, I am returned to my state of all-consuming solitude.

Branches loom through the sheer curtains of the bedroom windows, like outstretched arms, witch's talons. My mind turns to the militia and I wonder what its men could possibly find in this cloistered environment. Summer has reinforced its grip, delaying the arrival of autumn with its burnished browns and reds, the holly, thistles, hazelnuts and wild boar trails that follow in its wake.

My son's bedroom: his sheets and pillow, his smell, his clothes, his toys, the notebooks on his desk. Childhood smells like wheat fields. I'm drunk on Erwan. I picture him in the playground, waiting for his name to be called, his school bag on his back, dressed in his denim shirt, shorts and long socks, his Virgin Mary medallion against his skin. I don't believe in God, but I'm superstitious, I pray to ward off evil. My prayers are addressed to a higher power, to nature in our garden, where I cull and shape in vain. Nature resists me, our house does too, it's too vast for me, too cold.

Pink Floyd, *The Wall.* I dance, electrified. I long for a revolution of my own, I want to replace every cell in my body, break all my bones, whip up my blood, change my features, regain my youth. I'm waiting for someone, a stranger. I believe in the pre-existence of all things: stories that are written before they play out, the imprint of footsteps before they are taken, their path marked out, reserved. I'm swept along by the music, bathed in sweat. I feel sullied by Brahim's pleasure. We are unique and we are nothing.

I feel spied on by the masses, the crowd, I feel guilty for no reason, judged. Writing is my safety net. I, who constantly launch myself into space and stare into the abyss, convinced that I can soar above the city and my family without falling and injuring myself. I want my diary to be seen, I want it to be read by those I love, I want to be judged and punished by them, absolved, cleansed of my sins.

The lilac's branches are tied up in knots, it's suffocating. I should untangle them but I'm afraid of damaging the lilac's mechanism for producing the perfume that induces such headiness, obsession. I'm in love with my garden. The stone is hot beneath my bare feet. My body is cut off from Brahim's, without his hand around my waist, on my belly, my shoulders, and yet I'm certain of the pressure of a hand on my waist, on my belly, my shoulders. I lie beneath the palm tree from Bou Saada, absorbing the sun's rays filtered through its leaves, the light striated, deflected from its path.

Imagining Erwan has become my obsession; I look up at a passing cloud and my gaze meets my son's as he looks up from his desk to stare out of the classroom window, astonished to see the sky darkening. A few years ago, a plane flew overhead scattering advertising leaflets, triangular slips of paper that the children chased after thinking they were banknotes.

A memory: strolling in Paris with my brother – flowery dress, red heels, the bliss of aimlessly walking the city streets without fear of being spat at, insulted, stared at, my brother completely unaware of what I was feeling. My joy at reclaiming my feminine identity was marred by the knowledge that it would be lost to me again as soon as I boarded the plane, the Air Algérie flight that would bring me back here to my 'neuter' existence. Hidden behind my sunglasses, hat and loose clothing, I am not a woman here. I am a creature denied the advantages that men enjoy, the power they have over others; the city belongs to them. Even nature herself, for all her beauty and grandeur, is on their side. Women sometimes go to the rocks at Bérard to bathe, men go there to hide in the bushes and stare at them. It makes for a strange, unbalanced tableau – the men, hypnotised by the scene, the women, non-swimmers doing battle with the waves, unaware of the watching men.

Female nakedness is an offering, the body is not free; to walk in Algiers is seen as engagement with male desire, provocation.

In the garden, wearing only my nightshirt, I wonder what I would say if the militia men were to come and question me about the bottles of alcohol stored in the garage, the empty glasses on the steps to the terrace, the overflowing ashtrays, signs of night-time revelry, of artificial pleasures, a rarity here. I would shield Brahim, speak of my solitary drinking, pass myself off as a wayward woman who needs to be taken in hand, disciplined.

I spend more time inventing a life than living my own. I miss Erwan, he is caught up in a story that no longer involves his parents, the story of a schoolboy ready to learn, study, have fun. I envy him his childhood – mine comes back to me through smells, flashes of colour, disembodied voices. My past is a blur to me here; my memories, sifted through the passing years, retain neither gold nor precious stones.

Alcohol is for the evenings, my days are devoted to keeping order: tending plants, preparing meals, performing household tasks, cleaning to banish the shadows. On the terrace, in the bedrooms, the living room, the kitchen, I soap, scrub, rinse, hoping to wash away my ennui and become someone else, a woman running happily into her husband's arms, giving herself. Happiness is not something you can learn or earn. It's like intelligence, there is a predisposition for it, just as there is for ideas and their power. The sun beats down on my head but my place is in the shadows.

I wash myself without touching my body, scouring my skin with the washcloth – how easy it would be to take pleasure in the experience, but the image of Erwan holds me back. Meticulously, I remove excess skin, nails, eyebrows; my make-up is light, my features will be hidden by my glasses. I make an effort for my son, Brahim will think I've done it to please him, I won't disabuse him.

The body that must be tended to, as if it were imperilled. The body that must be perfumed, clothed: I select a beige linen dress, a light-coloured scarf, sandals, three fine, golden bracelets. I have an appointment. Rituals shared by all women. What image are we slaves to? My own image, reflected, is difficult to look at.

I have built my world on motherhood. It is my womb that has remained attached to Erwan and not the other way round. I must be sick, mad, I'm ashamed of writing this. Words can repair, like a needle and thread mending torn fabric.

I'm finding my role difficult, I don't know if I'm playing it right, if I'm too close to my son. I feel I am his skin's skin, that he is the extension of my childhood whose details I have lost. I want his childhood to be memorable, I work hard to make it so – our outings, our sea swims, the Christmas tree we cut down in Baïnem Forest, the fields, the '*petit*' desert just outside the city. I have only the beauty of the landscape to give him. What will he remember of the colours of the rocks, the sand, the valleys cut through by oueds, by raging waters full of dangers?

Perhaps the abiding memory of his childhood will be one of dissonant love. Erwan knows about me and Brahim. He witnesses the spectacle of our failings nightly, he goes to sleep with this reality.

Impossible to cut a wisteria flowerhead, to enclose it in a vase. It fades immediately, destroyed by the toxic atmosphere I spread through the house.

My time must be occupied, used. I would lose myself in sleep otherwise, with the help of barbiturates, alcohol. I have no suicidal feelings, I know just how much to take; I go no further than the first stage of intoxication, far enough to undo a thread, loosen the knot of anxiety, free myself without becoming completely detached from reality. I am mastering the art of not sinking too far.

When I imagine myself escaping, I see myself driving my car, heading for the palm groves of Timimoune, an African setting, made of the red earth of Sudan, an ultimate refuge; I dream of its splendour, so different from the city of Algiers. A place where men are reclusive, sleeping, shadowy, where women control their own lives, their shared existence. A matriarchy that rules over the village rituals, its economy, ensuring the survival of all, like the water wheels that irrigate the crops, that improbable display of nature's bounty in the depths of the Sahara. No one will find me there, no one will be able to join me. In my imagination, I am without Erwan. I extract him from my mad imaginings and remain a *good* mother.

I make a cherry tart. It must be crisp but not burnt, filling and crust perfectly balanced, the custard keeping its shape in the hot oven and blending with the caramelised crust without making it soggy, the fruit turning dark brown through the juice-splattered glass panel, like eyes staring up at me, tiny frogs swimming on the surface of the still liquid custard.

I go to pick up my son, dressed in a summer frock, wearing perfume. I feel 'womanly'. As I write this, I realise how it could be interpreted. But it's not carnal desire I feel for Erwan, it's jealousy, an unnatural jealousy of those who will steal his heart from me. Time is on my side. The loyalty of childhood that has such an effect on me works in my favour. I'm afraid of shaming him, I've said this before. I must seduce him if I am to seduce other people.

My notebook and my pen in my bag: a weapon and a round of ammunition.

I lock the door to the garden, go through the garage, the car is outside, I check to see if anyone is watching; I feel expected, but I've lost that sense of danger. Summer is unending in Algiers, the heat goes on, dense, unbroken beneath a less brilliant sky.

'*Salama, salama, salama.*' I greet the neighbours at their windows, on the steps of their houses. 'The sad French woman,' I know this is how they refer to me.

The honeysuckle's perfume energises me.

I drive fast, the radio is playing the Arabic song that Brahim translated for me, the story of a man in exile whose only solace is the shade of a tree that reminds him of his country, of 'childhood's hanging garden'.

My beige dress hangs like a sack on me, it's too baggy, I feel out of time, in disguise, not well 'turned out', as my mother would say, not at all like the fashion models I gaze at admiringly in women's magazines. Elsewhere, women are making lives for themselves, taking advantage of the sexual liberation I've only seen on album covers – Boney M., Donna Summer, Cerrone.

I sit in the car waiting for my son. He'll come running towards me, he'll press his face to my chest, reunited with 'his' leading lady, me, in my supporting role, in the background, blending into the décor, the cardboard landscape.

A group of children play football with a Gloria milk carton, some of them barefoot, boys set loose in the streets that can be fatal if a trolleybus speeds by too fast. My fascination for these flocks of children disturbs me. I compare their lives to my son's; their happiness amid such poverty fills me with sadness.

I hear the school bell, picture Erwan collecting his things, leaving the classroom, eager to get back to me, apprehensive of not being to find me in the throng of mothers.

A thought intrudes suddenly, of me disappearing, of my son searching for me in the forest of schoolchildren and finding himself left alone in the street, then joined by the street children who surround him, jostle him, help him to look for his mother. Like a sentence erased by the magic marker that whites out ink and makes it fade into the paper, I could simply vanish into the earth.

The clamour of schoolchildren, boys and girls, running down the stairs of the Hydra school, the rumbling of engines from double-parked cars, the hubbub and bustle all make me anxious. Everything spills over with life and youth – the air in the school gardens filled with the perfume of flowering hedges, the familiar school building, a remnant of colonial days with its courtyard, cloakrooms, patio and, upstairs and at the far end of the corridor, Erwan's classroom.

Erwan isn't alone, there's a boy at his side. They come down the stairs, talking, shoving each other. The boy gives him something. I can't make out what it is at this distance. Erwan stuffs it into his shorts pocket. A column of air surrounds them, a gap in the light that stops them from falling despite their pushing and shoving, the excitement of a shared secret.

Erwan has become more self-assured, because of the boy perhaps, or maybe it's simply being away from us, from me, that's made him shoot up suddenly, like a plant stimulated by intense, continuous ultra-violet light.

The boy is slight, like Erwan, the same height, identically dressed in shorts, shirt and white basketball shoes. Straight hair, streaked with blond, in contrast to Erwan's thick, dark curls. He has the bronzed tan of someone who's spent their summer holidays in the open air, not hiding from summer's onslaughts like us. I'm struck by his beauty, alarmed by it, imprisoned as I am in melancholy, secretly longing to draw Erwan into the trap with me to avoid losing him.

I'm witnessing the forging of an alliance, I can sense it. Erwan is my skin, I've written this before, I know how important the boy in the white basketball sneakers is; the smallest thing could transform him into the hero, the centre of the universe, chosen by the sun and the schoolchildren cheering him on (in my deranged imaginings). He's popular. Erwan has chosen him as a way of escaping me. The boy has selected Erwan as his companion, his sidekick (still in my ravings), the one he'll cause to suffer from unrequited love.

With every thought I'm forced further into my solitary state, I'm jealous of a child who will make my child happier. Like me, Erwan hasn't made any real friends here.

As they come closer, I can see they're holding hands.

The boy is very 70s: his haircut, his style, the ivory neck-chain. I'm old hat, I don't stand a chance. I'm not the main character any more, I'm the rival. His beauty is mercurial, two faces in one, merging, chasing each other away, alternating; a changeable beauty that is more animal magnetism than true beauty. He'll hurt Erwan, I should protect him. My jealousy is unleashed, I'm powerless against it, I realise what is happening but I can't stop. I'm sure the boy will see it in my face.

He introduces himself, his name is Bruce; I introduce myself and he says: 'I know who you are' and walks away, without a word to Erwan. He opens the door to a black Citroën CX, the car used here by officials; the driver won't get out of the car to greet him, kiss him.

Erwan unwraps the foil package containing a slice of still warm cherry tart. I drive in silence, with no music, staring at him in the rear-view mirror, his lips red from the fruit. I feel a slight sense of disgust at the sound of him chewing.

The trees lean in over the road, bending to form a guard of honour for us, two mute passengers. I concentrate on the road home, I don't stop to pick up a parcel at the post office,

I'm paralysed, stupefied, intimidated by Erwan; he's spent a whole day without me, he hasn't missed me.

I turn the dial on the radio, searching for the Italian station we can get on clear days, I need the sound of foreign voices as I ask shakily about his new friend.

Bruce is a girl, not a boy; she worships Bruce Lee. Bruce is a nickname.

She calls my son The River because he was crying this morning. I'm sure I was looking up at a cloud at the same time, I sensed his sadness over the rooftops, the walls between us.

The new equation – Bruce, strength, Erwan, fragility – is pushing me out of the story.

They've found one another, or rather Bruce has found in Erwan the opportunity to exert her power. My son is no match for it, he can't stand up to it, tainted as he is by my melancholy, that malevolent force that yields only to fear. Erwan will submit to her power, worse still, he'll lose himself in Bruce's personality, in admiring her, emulating her. I feel dispossessed; Bruce is a child, I try to picture how she has arrived at this point, defining herself in this way, giving the impression she gives, defying me with the self-assurance of a person armed with the weapons to defend herself.

I think longingly of our summer, believing I've lost a part of Erwan. My jealousy is either a delusion or a form of self-protection. I lock Bruce away in my notebook. Something emanates from her face and body, the intimation of something nascent, inevitable. I feel compelled to write it down, confine it. She is the raging torrent that will drown out The River, Erwan.

I'm naïve enough to believe that words have the power to act as a dam, that writing has magical qualities that can protect what I commit to the pages of my notebook from misfortune and cast spells on those who wish us harm. I am Erwan's mother, Bruce should not forget this.

I give her no quarter. I don't know her at all, but she is my sworn enemy. I'm haunted by Bruce.

Her eyes, lips, teeth are all oversized, prominent, out of proportion with her face. No sign of femininity, no breasts, hips, belly or thighs that I can recall. I watched her as she walked away, with X-ray vision, fascinated by her bearing, the look she had invented for herself, her gait, every stride lifting her in the air, propelling her towards the waiting car.

The football players were watching her too. I remember hearing the word 'ataï', faggot, as she walked by, probably because of the necklace.

Legs, like matchsticks attached to her pelvis. She's slender, narrower than Erwan, spiky knees and elbows, ribs protruding visibly no doubt under her shirt.

Her hair is cut like Les Poppys, Erwan's favourite band.

Her look, sad and insistent.

The creases in her shorts and blouse, carefully ironed and starched. Her watch, a man's, a diving watch.

I reconstruct the scene, Bruce is standing in front of me, ready to slap me (my madness). I'm transferring my violence onto this child, obsessed by the fear of losing my son, of being defeated by a friendship formed only a few hours ago.

The driver of her car was probably watching us in the rear-view mirror, making sure of Bruce's effect on us; the charm worked instantly, our skin was scorched.

Bruce has already left an empty space that I fill by replaying the scene.

The sky is yellow. A Polaroid image taken from above would reveal the multicoloured roofscape of the teeming, stifling city. Algiers could melt into the beauty of the sky, but like an organism poisoned by its own blood, the city resists.

I feel watched, spied upon, imagining that someone has given a signal to the men of Algiers, instructing them to leave the port district and make their way up towards Hydra in search of me, to beat me and kidnap me.

Images of tortured bodies linked to a film, its title forgotten but not its disturbing effect. The main character, a Christlike figure, being whipped by women, taking pleasure in the pain, a character I identify with.

On the way back to our house, we pass students wearing hijab, Brahim calls them Khomeiny's nuns, he's convinced it won't catch on, it will pass, Algeria is not Iran. He's wrong. The 70s are a decade of fire for us, nothing can stem the flames.

They say here that souls in agony rise weightlessly to heaven, like ashes carried on the wind.

My fear of losing Erwan leads me to think of tragedies, tales of life and death – like our relationship. It's unhealthy, I know.

Or perhaps Bruce has come at the right time. What if her appearance were to force me to be open to new influences, make me rise to a situation that gave me no choice but to emerge from my solitude, my melancholy? To bow to her?

I need a glass of wine to blot out this boy-girl I've just met.

The garage door is open, I'm certain I closed it. I say nothing, give the house keys to Erwan, who is eager to get back to his room, his things. I inspect the garden: clumps of soil turned over, plants trampled, by an intruder perhaps, or simply by insects and worms, a signal from nature of the damp days to come, of the season of moss, ferns and fungi.

A salamander slips under the wall, disappearing into the structure of our house, home in my imagination of forbidden thoughts, of my regrets, dreams of escape, the childhood I hardly think of any more. My adult self has erased its innocence. All I see are images of the brother I've stopped calling, envious of his tales of his eventful life in France, while I squander my youth here in this aimless existence. My future is a void.

I make some toast for Erwan, he's still hungry, mix him some chocolate milk, open a bottle of wine for myself, just one glass, enough to calm my nerves – a single dose, an injection of sugar, cotton wool.

My son, sitting on a branch of the medlar tree, helping himself to the fruit and flinging the stones over the wall into the garden next door, his favourite game. I'm in his room, picking up his things, his satchel, pens and paper, his shirt and shorts. He's changed clothes, I rifle through his pockets, nothing there. I tidy away his books and notebooks, see the piece of paper on his desk: '60 14 90 Bruce Shell Building'.

Sitting on the terrace steps, we gaze admiringly at the leaves that will soon fall, the display of colours in the garden – our flowers are still miraculously intact after the summer's heat – the new row of grasses I've put Erwan in charge of in an effort to pass on to him my love of nature. I want him to be aware of what nature gives us, of what she could take away from us; I'm passing my fear of being submerged onto him too, the dream that's haunted me the whole time I've lived here, of a great wave engulfing the city in the aftermath of an earthquake. Beauty leads me towards death, I can't help it. It's an illness, melancholia. I should be glad, for this reason alone, that Bruce has come into Erwan's life.

Bruce must have demons of her own, she must be haunted by the dream of becoming someone else, a different person. She's taken control, before adolescence can betray her and take possession of the body I suspect she keeps in check with such care and attention.

'She's not like other girls,' Erwan says. I clasp him to me, his cheek against my skin, his smell of rubber, glue, crayons, his piping voice, my little boy.

Higher up, the shadow of the Shell building standing like a many-legged monster on its piers, ready to stir into action and advance towards us, crushing everything in its path. Its balconies are empty, dry, sterile, as if the people living there were no match for the surrounding gardens, a defensive wall of hedges, eucalyptus, clusters of dark mimosa that spill over like swarms of hornets into the street.

Erwan hands me the object Bruce gave him, a metal sheriff's badge, engraved with the words Washington, DC. I rub the star against the fabric of my dress: 'to make it shine like all the other stars,' erasing Bruce's features, casting an evil spell.

I miss Brahim, I need his physical presence, I need his body to replace the body of my child, the body that is destined to betray me. Once, I'd believed we were alone in the world, but there is no place for me in Erwan's future. I need Brahim's firm hand to overpower Bruce's, his strength to lift me and carry me to our room. I crave his gentle touch to send me to sleep, hoping never to wake again.

Daylight has faded, the birds have vanished, Erwan lights the lanterns and I go inside to make our dinner.

Olive oil on the raw meat.

Thyme and bay, garlic and onion, herbs and leaves to garnish mortal remains.

The tajine dish: a sarcophagus.

Discomfort at the sight of the slaughtered beast, the discomfort of transgression, getting ready to devour a fellow creature.

Wine. Rows of vines stretching out like towns across the valleys, still authorised, protected, the grapes heavy, sensuous, staining the earth and the arid rocks.

Wine. A landscape that works its way into me and leads me back to the edge of happiness.

Tonight I shall give myself to Brahim, to the phantom beings I imagine as we make love. Our sexuality tells an alternative version of our story, like a dream that shows us a different reality and then retreats, taking with it the images that gave it life, leaving us to our dread, our stupor, unable to understand what we have seen.

The phone rings, I pick it up, silence, the empty silence of a line in use. I imagine Bruce at the other end, on the top floor of the Shell building, floating in the sky. Her face is not the face of the child I met this afternoon. It's the face of the man at the beach.

I hear Brahim's car, his footsteps, he joins me in the kitchen, leans on my shoulder, grasps my hips, kisses the back of my neck, the automatic gestures of a lover repeated a thousand times, to which I offer no response, my body frozen, ashamed of not loving his gentleness, secretly wishing for violence.

He pours himself a glass and heads for the bathroom.

I think of the anonymous call. I know I need to get closer to my son's father.

Brahim, squatting in the bathtub, washing himself with the shower hose. His right hand sliding over his body, he lathers the dark patch of pubic hair, lingers over the creases as he soaps his belly, chest, armpits, his back from high to low. He stands up, rinses himself off, eyes closed. I gaze at him without admiration, despite the well-formed muscles, buttocks, penis, the sturdy frame and statuesque shoulders, the body I have held so many times to my breast only to lose myself in fantasies of cruel men, commanding lovers.

I want to embrace him, walk away leaving him aroused, give myself some sense of importance.

Nipples, darker beneath their protective fuzz than the area surrounding them, the areola expansive, reminiscent of a woman's breast.

Toes spread, water running through them, like miniature sluice gates opening and closing with the force of the flow.

Thighs not built for swimming but for walking, climbing, running – Brahim is a man of the earth, of roadways and high plateaus.

Watching him lost in concentration as he bathes, I'm moved; I used to think of us as conjoined twins, with one heart, breathing with one breath. Our youth has gone and with it the pledges we made, I could so easily be unfaithful to him, I am unfaithful, already, in my thoughts.

His expression when he realises I'm looking at him, his smile full of the innocence I've lost.

He draws me to him, wraps the towel around me, draping me with cool, damp, perfumed flesh. He kisses me, I count to six and pull away, he doesn't stop me, out of weariness, resignation; I resent him for not restraining me, if I were to leave the house, the country, he'd do nothing to stop me, he'd be defeated before the battle, the explanation, he wouldn't fight. When Erwan was in his third year of primary school there was a story going around about a French woman, another parent, who wanted to leave the country with her little girl to get away from her violent husband; she asked among the other mothers for one of them to lend her a passport for her daughter, she'd change the photo, she said and return the passport as soon she'd crossed the frontier, once she was safe in France. I remember thinking that if Erwan had been a girl, I'd have helped her; lending my child's identity like that would have made me believe that I was fleeing, that we were running away.

The weight of Algerian soil on French women's shoulders, a tunnel with no escape, we run along it, flailing.

Men don't have to experience the abuse, the grasping hands on dresses, skin, clammy hands, blackened with dirt, coal.

Male beasts. The city is a zoo, the houses are cages, females, all of us, are prey, Thomson's gazelles, stalked by predators and hunters.

Men experience a different form of violence: murder on the streets, being struck by axes, knives, stones if the killer is a child.

I tell Brahim about Bruce, he doesn't seem shocked by the creature I describe to him, disdainfully referring to her as 'the thing' (my jealousy), as if her being neither a 'real' girl nor a 'real' boy were a failing, a fatal flaw in their friendship. I'm ashamed of the words I utter, but Brahim pays no attention, my words don't exist for him.

I set the table, serve the meal and go out to the garden, I'm not hungry. I leave them together, father and son, I don't want to hear about Erwan's first day at school, or his description of his new friend; Bruce's name will come up at the end, the final flourish of the firework display. Erwan has understood that I'm jealous, he's playing with it, taking revenge for our solitary summer: the couple we formed, our two bodies in thrall to nature and my demons. Erwan probably thinks Bruce will rescue him from me.

Wanting to disappear into the boughs of the trees and never come back to Brahim and Erwan. To burrow down into their roots and run through the wartime tunnels beneath the city, with their damp walls, foul water, rats — anything to avoid hearing Bruce's praises sung.

Wanting to shout: 'You don't even know her.'

The house illuminated, silhouettes of my husband, my son, empty bedrooms, the living room through the sliding glass doors; I feel like a burglar gazing in admiration at her victims before holding them to ransom. In the night air the scent of jasmine is more invasive, heady, corrupt, the blooms turning to poison in the hands of anyone trying to pluck them. I'm drunk on wine and envy, I have neither the youth nor the beauty that Bruce has, nor am I the woman my husband expects.

Erwan has pinned the sheriff's star to his T-shirt. Bruce's father brought it back from America where he often goes for work. Glorifying Bruce's family. Enough of this, I must grow up, my son is more mature than I am: he's made a friend while I do nothing but talk to my plants, to the fish I'm about to gut and cook, to my pies as I watch them rise, golden and magical through the oven door.

Housewife.

Good mother, bad mother.

Lover of imaginary lovers.

Woman whose clothes are too big for her.

Brahim's insistent hands; after his bath he lets me know he's aroused, it makes me uncomfortable, he's too direct, too 'real'; in my mind I see only him, no one else slips into the space between us, my orgasm will be faked, I shall feel as if I'm betraying myself.

Words work perfectly, they leap from my thoughts to the page. I create a copy of the real world, constructing a house that's not ours, inventing a family that's not mine, confusing my notebooks and reality. The more I write, the more we become holograms of ourselves.

The disease of writing is like a fit of anger that's impossible to shake off.

I've stopped writing letters to my family, my parents, my brother; my journal comes first, a fire laying waste to the landscape, reducing it to ashes. My family have ceased to exist, they're hidden behind France, the country that is distancing itself from the continent of Africa, forgetting us. I'm pinning my hopes on the job at the lycée, I have faith in institutions, symbols: the Alliance Française, the cultural centre, the embassy. Places to seek refuge if revolution were to break out. We'd be first in the line of fire: Brahim, the traitor, me, the foreigner. We'd be forced to leave. I couldn't do it, I have neither the courage nor the strength. My flesh is bound to the soil of Algeria's flowers.

The air has the softness of an Indian summer. I check the garden gate, the garage door.

The garage is filled with detritus of our past. The air in here is hot, from the car engines as we park, the hot water pipes, the boiler. I think of it as a holy space, a central lung feeding us air, energy, magnetism, the reservoir of all the water that flows through the house.

I feel the presence of the Shell building, as if it were a giant on the hill, I feel its thousands of windows sparkling, the people who live within its wall, Bruce. The day will come when Erwan will go there and be lost to me. The surrounding forest is dense, resinous, they say couples go there to act out their desires, like pariahs condemned by the town, expelled. Nature is the only mother here, in her beds of leaves flesh is worn down.

Erwan asleep on the sofa, arms crossed on his chest as if to protect his sheriff's badge. I must outflank Bruce, take her by surprise, suggest to Erwan that he invite her over, I'd rather have them here where I can watch over them. Better than having them concealed within that curving modern structure that defies both city and sea with its alien grandeur. But then I abandon my plan, I can't bear the thought of Bruce in my garden, climbing the trees, trampling the flowers.

In the lilac-hued darkness before dawn, I hear the crackle of moths' wings burning as they fly into the still-lit lanterns, and from further down the street, a sound like a muffled gunshot. Algiers opens out, spreading in a new direction, revealing a topography hitherto unknown.

'One day something will happen,' I say to myself silently as I begin the pretence. Brahim presses his lips to my belly, my thighs, my sex.

In the morning I take Erwan to school, hoping he'll run into Bruce. There's no sign of her. She must be late, or maybe her driver dropped her off early on his way to another appointment. I watch Erwan climb the steps with the other schoolchildren (who don't speak to him, don't pay any attention to him) and imagine him running up to Bruce, throwing himself into her arms. I speed away, unable to face up to the tableau I've just imagined. It's all unbearable, me outside the school, my son inside with the Other.

I'm not sorry we didn't see Bruce, it makes me hate her though, she is imposing her absence on me, staying out of sight, as if I'm not worthy of her.

After school I drive down towards town, I drive fast, free-wheeling, alone, Brahim is at his paper factory, Erwan in class. I could disappear, take the motorway to the desert, towards Niger – is anyone thinking of me at this moment? No one is.

At the post office in Hydra, a package from France, perfume, children's clothes, a tennis game for Erwan to plug in to the television, a letter from my mother – I'll look at it later. People have no idea about our lives here: they don't realise that we're not free, that our phones are tapped, that we can't talk about politics, the new religious militia, the people who disappear; they know nothing of what's silently occurring here, of what we have to put up with. No one is aware that youth has been shattered, never to return. The sea is a barrage against the rest of the world; we are isolated, impoverished.

The sky is chequered with clouds, bands of white forming geometric shapes, breaking apart and coming back together again, reconfigured by a higher power.

I walk beneath the arcades of the Boulevard Zirout Youcef, towards the fisheries. Men's voices, the dockworkers, smells of crude oil and fish, the sun falling obliquely on the quaysides, the containers, the nets, the intense activity revives my will to live. I feel suddenly light, safe, here in the savage beauty of my beloved Algiers, deep in this forest of men who pay me no attention, men going about their tasks, drunk on light, exhausted from their labours. The sea fractures the sun's rays as they cast their light on the water.

Brahim's willingness to submit makes me feel even sadder. I find it impossible to look up to him, my lack of admiration for him reflects on me, and yet once upon a time he was the one I chose among all the Algerian students in France. I used to find his gentleness comforting, now it's a fault.

Released from my fantasies, the dockers go about their work, driving cranes, hauling goods, piling crates and containers onto palettes and securing them with chains. Their bodies are blackened from smoke, glistening with sweat.

My dual personality: the woman and the anti-woman who seeks out difficulty, craves it, who needs violence to feel the blood flowing in her veins. Disgusted with myself, I leave the port and go back to my car. My white blouse is stained, I've been sweating. I can hear my heart beating, my insides churning. I could offer myself right now to the first person to come my way. I am a damned soul.

I live a life of fantasy, I never act.

In the countryside outside Algiers, nature is gentle, measured, on my scale. I lie down in a field of poppies – red flowers, green grass – I'm in love with the soil, with the cracks in the mud as it dries, with the song of the nightingale, the taste of mint leaves, anise, the wind spiralling as it rises and cools the air, the scent of wood, the bushes, the thickets, the dry vegetation that crackles when fire takes hold.

I am the fire that sparks no flames. I am nature's twin, as gentle as she is, as violent when crossed.

White blouse, blue skirt, red pumps, I've unwittingly dressed in the colours of the French flag.

Lying down, looking up at the sky, I feel dizzy; I'm falling backwards into the sky above. A column of ants runs from my ankle up my left calf. Nature is my fortress.

Bites from the ants leave spots of blood on my skin. I'd rather give myself up to the insects than to Bruce's (imagined) cruelty.

I'd like to be able to say 'I love you' to myself – I can't do it, I've never been able to – and yet I think it's important to be able to declare one's love for oneself, freely, from the self to the self.

Brahim thanked me yesterday after he had finished, as if he'd made use of me, my body, the utensil – we've done this so many times.

How long has it been since we've said to each other: 'I'm in love with you'?

The wearing effect of time, love's forgetting, the idea of death ever present.

Awareness of tragedy is the end of the dream, of poetry.

To dwell constantly on death is to nourish a great sorrow, a deep despair.

I'm jealous of Bruce, of what she is, of her vigour. I'm jealous of the mother who gave birth to her and is bringing her up so free and untamed. Who is this woman? Erwan is so conventional. A child should be an enigma. I envy Bruce's mother. It shames me to write these words.

I drive back up towards the city, to Place d'Hydra, boulangerie, butcher's shop, the capable housewife, an automaton, not a woman in love. My body is transparent, I feel inhabited by other people, like a character in *The Invisible Man*. Algiers denies me any status. My role lies in the home, my sensuality resides in nature, in the trough of the waves; how can I forge a connection between what I feel and what I show to others? I need to open myself up, I'm in hiding.

Seeing Erwan and Bruce together for a second time confirms my suspicions: this friendship will wreak havoc. I'm afraid

Erwan will fall in love, it would be like falling in love with a boy – the thought unsettles me. Bruce's two faces, girl and boy, are traps for my son, they lay bare a side of him that would remain hidden if Bruce were 'normal'. How narrow-minded I am, intolerant, unpleasant; I know these are all nothing but excuses, a way of keeping Erwan by my side. He is a replacement for the part of my heart that's missing.

Bruce doesn't approach me, as if she knows what I think of her, she waves to me from a distance, Erwan turns round, watches as she disappears into the waiting car. The driver doesn't get out. Bruce is kitted out in a military shirt and khaki shorts, white tennis shoes. Such slender legs, her thighs already shapely, her body slight but athletic, from physical exertion perhaps, or self-denial.

The Citroën glides towards the Shell building, a phantom vehicle driven by a mystery man or perhaps by Bruce's mother, who refuses to get out of the car. She's disdainful, just like her daughter: a superior creature capable of making one gender dissolve into another, like a chemist who has stumbled upon the formula for creating a unique individual, neither boy nor girl. I've never met a child like Bruce, she has invented a third identity – strange, fascinating, unsettling. I wonder what kind of mother can put so much trust in her child, what kind of mother gives her child free rein to allow her destructive side to flourish and invade like a hard, dry, fibrous growth with the stems and petals of prized blossoms. Bruce is the twine born of beauty, enchanting, twisted, spoilt. Her beauty leaves me cold, it scares me. Bruce has destroyed the promise of her charms.

I drive away from our house towards what I call the 'low town', the guts of the city nestling between the heights and the port, Rue Didouche Mourad. I want to buy Erwan a present from the Drugstore, the new toy superstore.

Jostled by the crowd of men, my son's hand in mine, we offer little resistance against the tide of bodies manoeuvring to stay out of the sun.

The Drugstore is a state-owned concern, opened to allay the frustrations of families, it will close down eventually for lack of trade, nothing survives here, only the wind on the rocks. I let go of Erwan's hand, watch as he walks towards the section with toys made of wood, metal, paper – educational toys. He chooses a kit in malleable plastic, a miniature skeleton to put together – in my delirium I see it as a metaphor for the death of our relationship.

The city centre, a wildly beating heart that has stolen mine. My emotions are stirred by the lives of all those men and women, struggling, grappling, breaking apart, coming back together in the Jardin d'Essai, an open-air greenhouse, exotic, rich in plant life like the illustrations from my childhood. The colour of the sky, a splash of orange-tinged ink, unchanging, compulsive, reviving some of my lost happiness – making me certain once again that something will happen.

We buy school supplies for Erwan in the Place d'Hydra. He seems distracted as he hands me a tattered piece of paper, a scribbled list of notebooks, pencils, measuring instruments – ruler, compass, set square – clutching his toy against his thigh, anxious to construct the little skeleton, the child in him very much alive. The River, in love.

Bruce has a French mother and an Algerian father too, perhaps that's why they've connected. On the way home I see every car behind us as the little Renault 8 of the man who followed us to the beach. My fears arise from a wrong I'm going to commit, I'm chastising myself in advance – bewitched by an unknown force. Women, as ever, the guilty ones.

Premonitions of the unknown? Or the ravings of a mother touched by other people's madness?

The walls of our house are a mass of lilac-coloured wisteria as wild as my thoughts; I leave it to run riot, eating into the paintwork, ruining the plasterwork. The garden is quiet, sleeping, the fronds of the small Bou Saada palm curve downwards, trying to connect with the earth.

Erwan asks for permission to use the phone, picks up the receiver without waiting for me to answer and dials. I know he's calling Bruce. I leave him alone and watch from the terrace; his back is turned, he doesn't say much. I'm too far away to catch the tone of their conversation but I can read it in his body language – embarrassment, laughter, impatience, silence – the snake, coiling, squeezing, suffocating. Erwan stands frozen. I imagine Bruce playing a musical instrument, chanting satanic verses, a snake charmer hypnotising my son from afar, from that vast modern complex with its curved structure that rises above the city, a landmark for planes at night, all the way down to our white house with its wrought iron fencing, our peaceful enclosure that Bruce will disrupt, pillage. She'll ravage the space of love and tenderness that I have created for my son, secure in the knowledge that it is better to be armed with gentleness than with violence – a belief that will surely come to grief. I was born under a star that no light can penetrate, but there is nothing to stop me wanting a better life for Erwan, hoping he will grow up to be a happy man who believes in his lucky star.

Chicken feathers smouldering over the flame of the gas stove, spreading the scent of charred flesh all over the house, aromas of shallots, bouquet garni, comforting smells that take me back to days in my childhood spent watching my mother cook, infusing the meat, fish, pastries and flour with the love she was unable to express in any other way – a love that was constrained, an unexploded bomb. I think of my mother as a tree with sawn-off branches, a tree unable to flower, maimed, deprived of the vocabulary of tenderness in her childhood; unbalanced as I am, I resisted, I did not repeat her pattern. I exploded the bomb and covered Erwan in gestures, words. Erwan, the adored one.

The taste of wine on my tongue, grapes from the sun-scorched, windswept hills of Mascara, charged with electricity from lightning storms, the land in turmoil. The wine runs down my throat, takes hold of me, floods me with pleasure. I am the grapes, the sugar in the fruit.

The chicken roasting in the oven: its skin, basted in its own fat and olive oil to make it crisp, puffs up, forms bubbles – I'm comforted by the illusion of domestic bliss, I am a mother with the family I've created.

The rustle of life to counter the songs of death.

Erwan in his room filled with Bruce's presence. I'm on my own, waiting but not waiting for Brahim; wine is my friend, a faithful, wise companion.

Listening to Electric Light Orchestra play 'Telephone Line' on our Hitachi hi-fi system. I think back to Erwan's phone call to Bruce, their mysterious, silent conversation.

Like Erwan, I want to fall in love.

My life of boredom, knitting the stitches of death. I have no wish to die. I am nothing but I draw comfort from the certainty that all of us here on this earth, in this world, are nothing.

We have to construct our life, make it our own, a work that is unique. Size and beauty are of little importance, what matters is that it is: life, ephemeral as a butterfly's brief existence, extended a little further but with the same outcome. All I'm constructing is a wall between Erwan and other people. I want so much to protect him – this is why I shall lose him.

Leech mother.

My dark thoughts multiply when I'm away from Erwan. Without him, I'm caught in a danse macabre, a skeleton waltzing beneath the ivy, where rats and spiders lurk.

Erwan is in his room, I dare not disturb him, he's growing up, he'll soon be a young man with his own circle of close friends.

I watch my chicken turning on the spit through the oven door. I baste it with garlic and lemon juice, break up the bouquet garni and sprinkle it over the dish without burning my fingers – expert gestures, practised so many times. I see it as a corrupted form of love for animals, a way of anointing, consecrating – a coating of thyme, bay leaves and sage, a dressing of fat, salt, spices – the creature dressed, embellished, my efforts focused on granting myself absolution for the sacrifice and feasting.

The thread that links my son to the meal I'm preparing for him – I am still his mother, his flesh – an attachment that Bruce will not be able to sever.

Beauty and squalor, the glory of nature and the pit of despair, opposing forces; a people's revolt against the government is brewing, while in this house an uprising is fomenting among members of our family. Algeria's history exerts its influence on us; we too are swept along on its turbulent currents.

Sitting on the steps of the terrace, I help Erwan put together the little skeleton. We start with the ribcage. I'm surprised by the great number of bones in our bodies. We have to heat the tips of the bones in the flame of a cigarette lighter to connect the ribs, spinal column, skull and pelvis. They soften, fuse together, bond. It's a delicate operation: the toy is of poor quality, the skeleton will collapse but Erwan doesn't seem to notice. Suddenly, he announces in a serious voice: 'I've called Bruce you know.' I say nothing.

Brahim is held up at the factory, he'll be late home. Erwan and I eat together, just the two of us; we don't mention school, which is starting in two days, or Bruce. We talk about the sky, how limitless it is, the impossibility of representing the infinite, the movement of waves, eternity.

We are a couple again, reunited, like a lizard with its severed tail restored.

Our relationship is inherently stronger than the love that threatens it — a stranger's affection is uncertain, a mountain to be scaled only to be driven back down the other side by the vertigo induced by the great height of the summit.

I'm alone in the garden, Erwan is sleeping. I turn off the lanterns, check the garage door. Brahim will park outside to avoid waking us; I can hear fireworks, children playing unsupervised, enjoying a freedom my son will never have.

The little skeleton we placed on the table in the living room has come apart, as if it had started to walk off while our backs were turned and fallen to pieces. Does an obsession with death mean that a break lies ahead? Or a rebirth?

I stand in front of the bathroom mirror, removing my make-up – eyes, lips, cheeks. My skin is in need of kisses, my hands of a body to embrace; internally I crave pleasure, release. I have become empty flesh, a body vacated and ripe for the picking, a skeleton ready for disjointing, the little toy from the Drugstore.

We leave the bedroom window open. I dream of the garden encroaching on the house, breaching the walls – roots, branches, tendrils spreading out, working their way into my flesh and flowering inside me.

III

On the road to Tipasa. As we leave Algiers behind, the sea comes into view; I'm ready to immerse myself in its waters and set my body back on course. Brahim, dressed in a blue shirt, thick-rimmed dark glasses, steering wheel in one hand, cigarette in the other, the Algerian male; he watches Erwan in the rear-view mirror, smiles at me, focuses on the road ahead. What thoughts are going through his head? My sadness has created a distance between us, he suffers it in silence, he never complains; perhaps he escapes into dreamworlds, where I'm not invited, to dance alone or with other women. I'm not jealous, it's not real. Our car carries us swiftly along, rounding one bend after another; there is no god to protect us, only the sky, the shapes in the clouds, angels with sky-blue eyes.

Hard-boiled eggs in the cooler.
Mouzaïa sparkling water, rosé wine.
Tomato and rice salad.
Blood oranges from the Place d'Hydra.

Watermelon, rounded and voluptuous – like a woman's belly.

Salt and pepper in paper sachets.

A knife for sea urchins.

Slices of lemon.

Bread.

Sugar and orange-blossom doughnuts.

The parasol with blue and yellow triangles.

The orange canoe with its paddle and foot pump.

A smell of rubber and sea mist.

Rock formations like small offshore islands.

The housewife, the woman fleeing, soon the swimmer.

I feel compelled to write it all down, hold on to all of it, I am out of step with reality, walking in the shadows of trees and monuments. Words bear witness to my experiences, my inventions – Polaroid snapshots of my thoughts, comforting me when I am unable to connect with normality. Like Bruce, I am a creature from a parallel, closed world. Bruce scares me as much as I scare myself.

Sometimes Brahim lays his hand on my thigh, then removes it of his own accord, all I've done is straighten my skirt; in the clear light of day our flesh is unresponsive, only night can stir desire, legitimise it.

I fantasise about not going back to Algiers, continuing instead along the coast road all the way to the end – it must end somewhere. I imagine water gushing from an African clifftop, fresh water turned to salt water on contact with seaweed and silt.

My son's hands on my neck, he could strangle me if he wanted to; I'd let him do it, I wouldn't fight back. Erwan can do whatever he likes but Brahim has no more rights, except for those I grant him, when I allow his desire to mingle with mine in our bedroom. Outside, in social situations, we display none of the sensuality of normal couples.

Summer's heat has scorched the trees and scrubland that separate the road and the ravine from the sea, sole object of my desire. Hawkers selling daffodils, daisies, wicker baskets hail us as we drive past, too fast to stop and buy. Brahim despises them, they carry his childhood in their hands.

Our sturdy orange canoe floating on the waves at Zeralda, Figuier, Chenoua. I think of men in flimsy crafts dreaming neither of glory nor fortune, driven only by the longing for freedom.

There is no freedom for me, inattentive as I am to the man I should cherish as I promised to do with our first kisses; I've gone back on my word, betrayed my youth, our future. Only the intervention of fate could wrench me from my lies and madness now. With every car journey I'm transported back to that first trip, when I left my native land for the country I was supposed to save, the country that was supposed to save me; who am I here?

The sea is like me, a woman belonging to no one, her many faces shifting and duplicitous. The Mediterranean, where madness reigns, unchanging in the face of storms. Oceans wash away their own footprints and remake themselves but the Mediterranean never retreats.

'The neighbours were questioned about us,' Brahim informs me. 'A man wanting to know if you went out to work, if you had any links with the French Embassy, if I spoke Arabic to our son.' The neighbours said they didn't know me that well, that we seemed like a quiet, family leading an uneventful life.

Joan Baez on the car stereo. Erwan thinks she's singing about love but the song is about anarchists: 'Here's to you Nicola and Bart, rest for ever here in our hearts.'

A stay-at-home mother and her political consciousness – I missed my chance to be involved, I traded it in for 'an uneventful life', as my neighbours put it. My youthful idealism will have to flower elsewhere, in a different form, fight a battle I can't name yet. Impossible to forget the call to rebel, the daggers of injustice, the blood of martyrs.

Impatiently, Erwan asks what time it is, he seems both anxious and happy, he's often like this, lost in the landscapes of childhood no longer familiar to us, meadows inhabited by witches and fairies, until adolescence arrives to impose the demands of the flesh, the perils of the heart. How I wish I could protect him from suffering, from the suffering we create for ourselves, the pain that others inflict on us.

A mirage shining on the road, a watery barrier that vanishes as we drive through it. Roman ruins emerge beneath the sheltering umbrella pines, the remains of an arena, as if a shell had exploded, showering rocks over the carpet of flowers beneath the trees, crowns of mauve, pink, white, crimson. Nature is History's cemetery; souls toss and turn amid the sleeping vipers, sucking moisture from the reeds, reigning over beetles and scarabs. Tipasa, a vision. Columns, baths, pillars, pipelines, stairs and towers, fragments of bowls, amphoras, vestiges of walls that have crumbled and rolled all the way to the edge of the beach where they stop, frozen in time, eaten away by fossils that cling to the fragments of the ancient city that was once a lookout point over sea and ships.

I imagine the sound of voices, the rush of bodies, the clang of arms, the crashing of waves throughout the long nights of waiting, the days filled with hope.

Our cove is secret, away from the well-equipped family section. The only access is by foot, a path beneath the trees, a small moist world of viscous resins amid the shrill cacophony of cicadas. We are stepping into the bedchamber of the Mediterranean. I have visions of naked bodies, their flesh caked with mud, pricked by pine needles, adorned with violet flower petals, bodies mingling, grappling, their lust resembling a battle. We walk in single file like a band of smugglers: Brahim at the head, me at the back, our son between us. We reach the ladder that leads down to the cove, Erwan climbs down onto it, his movements agile; he holds out his hand for me – he hasn't forgotten me yet. The cove has golden sands, sheltered from the wind by the rocks. The elements have constructed and honed an enclave known only to us, discovered one autumn as we searched off the beaten track for holly and thistles.

On the beach, Brahim's body is returned to me; his belly beneath my palms, his shoulders, I let him embrace me, his hands enclosing my body in silken shackles. I emerge from my darkness.

I dive into the sea. Floating on my back I go back to my beginnings, remembering my mother on a beach in Brittany, hands behind her back, scrutinising the horizon as if she were waiting for a sailor, for happiness, to return. What if she passed the sickness of melancholy on to me along with the colour of her eyes, her freckles, her athletic body? The watery depths below me teem with marine life, creatures weaving in and out of a space as densely populated as the city of Algiers. I imagine sunken craters, valleys of sand, mud holes, wrecks, bones, the drowned and the shipwrecked, ghosts of the sea.

I drift, listening to the sounds of my body, the internal symphony of heart, blood and breath, I could let myself be carried far out to sea, wash up on an island, start a new life and never return. Lost in my reverie, I don't hear Erwan calling me from the shore.

Birds fly in the spaces between the streaks left in the sky by airlines, their route to Africa marked out, a route that I too could follow if I had wings to fly away, to escape.

I close my eyes against the sun, arms outstretched, the water is warm. Brahim must be setting up our spot, anchoring the umbrella with rocks, spreading our immaculately laundered towels out on the sand. Dressed in his striped swimsuit, he looks like a Hollywood Robinson Crusoe, with his powerful, muscular thighs and buttocks, his beard and his thick, greying hair. Erwan, his partner in arms.

Our cove is a rare source of happiness in Algeria for me, a place where I can feel forgotten about and, therefore, safe. The beach is difficult to access, the path snaking through low-growing bushes, invisible from the main road. No peeping Toms hiding here.

Underwater, a fluid landscape of corals, seaweed like green hair tinged with bronze, dense moss clinging to rocks – fractured vaults of a kingdom besieged – sea urchins in abundance, reminiscent of chestnuts. I need oxygen. I resurface, swim towards the shore, still not hearing Erwan calling me, kicking my legs as if beating time as I swim freestyle at a steady pace, breathing to counts of two, hoping to inspire admiration in my son.

The cruellest betrayals are perhaps the ones we expect the least.

I draw close to shore and see that Erwan is not alone, he's with a child and a woman, he waves his arms wide, signalling to me. I recognise Bruce's silhouette, her face, her look of defiance. She's achieved her goal, Erwan has given her directions to our cove, she's won his trust.

'Catherine Bousba.'

'Michèle Akli.'

'You know my daughter, Bruce, I believe?'

'Yes, that's right.'

I don't know Bruce, I bow to her, to her strength, her hidden force. She has chosen my son. I can't fight it. Why Erwan? Why The River? Probably because he needs to be delivered from the strictures of childhood and because I don't have the courage to let him take flight. Bruce will do my work for me; she'll do a good job, I can see her being as meticulous with Erwan as she is with herself, disguised to perfection as she is.

Mother and daughter by the sea, two bodies made of quartz, skin sparkling with thousands of droplets running from shoulder to ankles. They've just been swimming, they arrived earlier, the leaves in the forest were still wet with dew, they'd thought they were lost until they found the ladder, and then they were stunned, dazzled. Such an unexpected surprise, a gift from the gods – the beauty of the place, of the sea that encloses it, a deserted island, a secret garden, sheltered from the wind and heavy swells by ramparts that are soft to the touch, rocks born of magma, polished by storm and wind. They chose a spot at the far end, not wanting to disturb us (lies), hidden behind a rock. I berate myself for not having seen them when they arrived, for not having prepared myself for this encounter, giving free rein to my discomfort, my fragility, my soul bared and disarmed. Catherine Bousba has seen through me just as Bruce did the day of our first meeting.

Ambushed.

I feel hatred towards Erwan.

Catherine, touching me on the shoulder (who does she think she is?), thanking me for the secret address.

What a good person I am.

Bruce, smiling that wolfish smile.

Nature dissolves around me, I need something to hold onto, a base to anchor myself, I stagger.

In the background, Brahim smokes beneath the parasol, watching the scene as if he were a minor player, a witness keeping his distance, acknowledging neither Bruce nor Catherine Bousba, waiting for my signal, anxious not to interfere in something that doesn't concern him, women's business, mothers' talk. Catherine has selected her target, Bruce hers. Erwan and I are in their hands.

Bruce has nothing of her mother's blonde actress-mother look. She reminds me of Catherine Deneuve, a look-alike with the same name, or maybe it is just because she's so beautiful. She has that 1970s look, her long hair cascading over one side of her face. She wears gold, fine chains around her waist, a plain wedding ring, small luxury watch, her nails are painted, fingers and toes, red beneath the clear water. Her costume is a black bikini, tied at the sides. Bruce leans into her, arm around her waist, her companion, her lover, her soldier – although this woman surely doesn't need anyone to protect her. She's already made her mark on the cove, the shoreline, and the Mediterranean too – she's left an imprint, like shellfish on the Roman columns.

Bruce is wearing tight-fitting shorts of mid-thigh length, her skin is dark, her face lighter than her body, her stomach is like a boy's, she has a better build than Erwan, for now (my jealousy).

My son – his arm not around my waist, his hand not in mine – gouges a hole in the sand with his foot, stirring up gravel and plankton, his way of blunting the perfection of our idyllic surroundings, embarrassed, not by Bruce but by Catherine Bousba, her dizzying perfection. Nothing about her is out of place, nothing is ungainly or uncertain, everything is harmonious; I could trace the smooth contours of her body, linking brow, collarbone, navel, hip, knee, ankle, like lines in a textbook between the planets — every part of her body the epitome of grace. She's neither tall not short, her body is built to be desired by men, by women, taking our breath away from that first look, showering us with handfuls of crystals and rose petals.

Actress-lover, rival, she plays a dual role, while I feel my body sinking into the damp sand, shrinking by inches, bowing to obey her voice, her blue eyes shot through with orange — Catherine Bousba, the extra-terrestrial and her boy-girl daughter. 'We're lost, Erwan,' I say to myself. Thirsting, held in thrall, shipwrecked. I need Brahim, I need him to rescue me, lead me back to him. I'll sit at his feet, on the bathmat, like a dog refusing to leave its master. But fate has intervened and I am defenceless. I've already left him.

Catherine dives in, followed by Bruce, a pilot fish attaching itself to her body, they swim out to sea together, Erwan follows in their wake, dog-like in his turn, unable to keep pace. They don't wait for him, don't turn back to look, they know they've won, they're laughing to celebrate their triumph, their laughter devouring the cliffs and the sky.

Algiers was hiding this woman and I didn't know.

All those times I've circled our garden, walked in the looming shadow of her building, over all these years.

Only wine can free me.

Under the beach umbrella, ousted from my throne, I watch, like a beggar on the beach, as the two swimmers come back towards the shore, towards Erwan sitting at the water's edge, a little boy looking even younger now. Brahim has understood, he smiles, thinking he is my strength. He'll fall too. I let him kiss me, play the man and the lover, trying to pick up the threads of our story, our lie that cannot be sustained. Our son comes running over to us, his back turned to the danger.

How sweet to have Erwan beside me, I'm not angry with him any more, I forgive him, he's so like me. Catherine and Bruce a few metres away, held in my vision as if in the sight of a gun.

Wine, watermelon, cracking pips between my teeth, the cove transformed, its hidden treasure revealed: the sun is out again, Catherine is stretched out on a rock offering herself to its rays, absorbing the light, taking pleasure in it.

Bruce's body is a mystery: this child has disrupted the natural order, reversed the direction of blood flow, overturned her birthright, created her own equilibrium, her second nature. I watch her skipping stones – well-defined muscles, powerful shoulders, fine bones: her bone structure gives her away, she must hate it. I laugh at the thought; this is how I weave my web of revenge, with venomous imaginings. Erwan joins her, she holds him by the scruff of the neck (the dog again), two boys arm in arm, an intolerable sight.

The wine holds me down like a straitjacket, stops me from getting up to separate them, to untangle their unholy alliance. Bruce is an alien being, I have no sense of her femininity, no image of it at all. She stands alone in the world, Erwan will be her subject, not her role model, she will experiment with my son's body and absorb his masculinity.

The sun moves across the sky, the people on the beach follow its arc, going about their business. Catherine gets up from the rock, Brahim leaves our beach umbrella, Erwan jerks away from Bruce's side, too suddenly. I pick up my snorkelling mask, net and knife and go in search of sea urchins.

Underwater, the world is magnified by my mask, I like it here more than on solid earth – mossy alcoves and fertile, uneven terrain, dark brown octopus, mother-of-pearl shells, organisms spitting out bubbles, molluscs with their yellow, viscous flesh – life, throbbing, blossoming, exploding, renewing itself, eternal.

The image of Catherine stays with me – her shapely body, suntan oil mingling with drops of water on her skin. I wonder what's happening up there on the beach. Maybe Brahim is moving closer to her, taking advantage of my absence, dragging her towards the damp forest, slapping her, roughly untying her bikini, attacking her to punish her for being there, for Bruce being there, for injecting me with menace and aggravating my melancholy.

When I surface to take a breath, I catch a glimpse of three silhouettes, clearly outlined, separate; all of them watching me as I dive down again. The sea urchins offer no resistance, I fill my net as they submit passively to being caught, heavy, plump, black, brown, purple, works of art. My haul of treasure will cause a stir. I want to seduce Bruce's mother – seducing a woman would be like seducing myself, I who feel no desire for my own body and am repelled at the thought of touching myself, of giving myself pleasure, I who despise any pleasure I feel.

Desires layered like a mille-feuille, two couples take shape in my mind: Erwan and Bruce, Catherine and me. The wine is unhinging me.

Brahim does not feature in my plan, he is lost. We are living the failed history of our two countries, the love affairs and burnt-out passions, I the French woman, he the Algerian man, I know they will live on down through the centuries, long after us. Once lands have been seized, there is no recovery.

Underwater, I think of Erwan swimming in my belly, umbilical cord encircling him, dependent, so longed for, the only child – he was all I wanted. I imagine Bruce, upright, unattached, a malevolent look on her face. People here say that squid ink sours a pregnancy, Bruce is a succubus, a creation of witchcraft. Beneath her resplendent exterior I imagine claws, hair.

I put down the net filled with sea urchins beside a rock that looks rather like a table. Brahim comes over to join me with wine, bread, lemons; Erwan and Bruce appear, followed by Catherine. We've tacitly agreed to share the feast. Something is beginning, I'm losing control, going along with it, the sun on my skin, my shoulder, my back, the nape of my neck, like a hand taking hold of me, ordering me to give in to my desire.

Brahim and Catherine don't need to be introduced, our children have brought us together. They face one another, adversaries at times (why?), accomplices at others. Brahim talks about Algeria, his Algeria, the mountains of Kabylia, the small village, the bitterly cold winters, nature's refusal to submit, the war and his departure, his love of paper (his factory), of literature, French culture. He grasps my hand and I withdraw it immediately, feeling ashamed, embarrassed to be the wife of a man I no longer love. Catherine speaks of her France, Paris, the connection she reforges several times a year, the arts, freedom, Europe. She tells of how she met Bruce's father, an oilman, one of life's chance encounters, of how she is 'tempted' by Algeria, such a colourful country when seen from afar, even more exotic when you live there, even though she feels as if she is passing through; she won't stay: 'the world is so vast, we have so little time.' Drawing Bruce towards her, she confesses that she is fascinated by this land with its new-found freedom, its political destiny: 'Great revolutions occur after the gunfire.'

I look away, catch her eye again, look down, stare straight at her once more. She's not the target any more, I've dropped the gun. I cut open the sea urchins – a sudden vision of little skulls being cracked open – I remove them from their shells, clean them, set them out on a platter, squeeze lemon juice over the flesh.

The hours pass, time is held in suspension, the heat, the smell of dried seaweed. Algiers has ceased to exist.

Catherine Bousba licks the inside of the shell, devouring the creature's body as if it were a woman, inhaling the blood-red corolla as if she were sucking out the essence of my being.

Passing around the wine, bread, lemon – shared pleasures – Catherine and I both conscious of what is at stake.

She addresses my son with disdain; Erwan must seem too clean-cut to her, a calm, well-behaved little boy, the only interesting thing about him in her eyes is probably his budding fascination for her daughter. 'So Erwan, last year of primary school?' I can see she thinks he's too small, too skinny and immature with his sailor cap and his fishing rod. My wonderful son.

Rivalry between mothers, females (how banal).

She moved Bruce to a new school, she was at the Golf School before, she wasn't happy there.

I imagine Bruce as the bully, scaring away the other children, pushing them around, or else as the victim, being spat on, having stones thrown at her.

Our children play by the water's edge. Bruce tells Erwan to dig the foundations of their castle deeper, my son follows her instructions. If Catherine were to tell me to kneel, to lick her stomach, I, too, would obey.

The freedom induced by wine, images rising unbidden in its wake and filling me with dread: of Erwan and Bruce playing sexual games, a tableau that violates nature. I vow to remain vigilant, to step in if they go too far, if my son is in danger.

And what if Bruce's nature were to spill over into Erwan's?

Brahim wades deeper into the water, crouches down and makes breaststroke motions with his arms — a touching sight. I look away hoping Catherine hasn't realised my husband doesn't know how to swim. With Bruce and her mother here I'm merciless, their presence has the same effect as my diving mask — faults stand out more, new ones are revealed.

This woman's skin, its heady perfume infused with the smell of moist underarms, her salty blonde hair, the folds of skin at the back of her neck. She swims, head underwater, I imagine her stomach between the surface and depths, tensed, cutting through the contours of the waves.

Brahim inflates the canoe for the children, lost in thought, cigarette in one hand. I wonder if he is unsettled by Catherine's beauty, if he's as ashamed of me as I am of him, of us, the ill-matched couple.

My desire will be postponed, put aside until a few days after the scene at the cove, to detach it from its source (the place, Catherine), cut it off at the roots to avoid seeing it for what it is: something new, strange, out of place. I've never been attracted to women, I'm indifferent to them usually, I don't actually want this woman; this is something else, behind this desire for her lies a longing for freedom, beauty, intoxication.

The measured tones of Catherine Bousba's voice, a dance of words, a symphony of sentences.

Words on the page don't have the power of film. They can't reproduce a person's physical being, the sounds they make, the contours of their movements; only a moving image can recreate an action in all its fullness.

The frustration at the heart of these notebooks.

Catherine's sterling-silver lighter, the way she lights her cigarettes, head bent, cigarette between her fingers, menthol ultra-light. Smoke coils in front of her eyes, little souls floating up to heaven.

The canoe is afloat, Bruce at the front wielding the paddle, the captain of the ship. Behind her, Erwan submits, taking orders as they navigate the waters between two cliffs: a sensory passageway to a new world that has no substance, a world that must be imagined, the only escape from the deathly ennui of life here. Erwan will stare into the depths hoping to discover a wreck while Bruce will put on a show of strength for him, standing up to row, braving the currents and the open sea.

Catherine is sleeping, or pretending to, while I watch over our children out on the water. The cove will no longer be our secret, I feel dispossessed, as I did the day I met Bruce, when I understood within a few seconds the nature of her plan: to take possession of my son, to change him and give him back to me diminished, damaged (my madness).

I can't get away from the feeling that someone wants to harm me, that I'm being spied on, that someone is waiting for me; the voice of my conscience perhaps, watching me, punishing me for my malicious thoughts?

Catherine gets up, takes a white shirt out of her bag, a man's shirt that she wears as a dress, cinched at the waist by a leather belt. She brushes her hair, knots it without the help of any pins, a whirl of unruly locks.

She steps onto the rusty little ladder, disappears from view behind the rock. Her laugh, again. She couldn't care less about me; I fear for her, I'm a danger to myself, I could be to her too. I'm worse than the men of Algiers, worse than the city that is engulfing me, a woman on the road to ruin.

In those leaden moments, after the effects of the alcohol have worn off, I look at Brahim, the man, on his knees using a pebble to smooth the towers of the sandcastle. Thousands of kilometres lie between us, from Tipasa to Brest. My memory is locked and bolted, a mausoleum; my French family have ceased to exist, I never think of them, they are laid to rest within me.

On the water, an orange dot that contains my son and his assassin.

I go in search of seaweed – large, fresh, shining pieces – to put on our garden, to fertilise the soil and make the young broom and mimosa trees grow tall and strong. Catherine Bousba's perfume in the air, *Must de Cartier*.

My one-piece swimsuit under the umbrella, neatly folded, my long skirt, my flowery blouse – I feel uncomfortable in my own skin, in my clothes, in my mind. My femininity has evaporated. I walk over to join Brahim, I want to address him as 'my darling', but no words escape my mouth. The sandcastle, a fortress we are building with our hands, to protect Erwan from Bruce.

I imagine Catherine lost in the forest, victim of an attack, I see her lying among the ferns, a trickle of blood at her lips, her shirt torn and tattered, the dense foliage her coffin, then I see myself as the attacker, taking her violently, replacing Brahim in my fantasy. I adopt the role of women's enemy, placing myself beside the bloodthirsty lovers of my dreams; my frustration is immense. I am worthless, I hate these thoughts.

The sky is pale yellow, summer is receding, time is an arrow propelling us towards a terrifying future. Catherine and Bruce are part of our lives, we won't be able to extricate ourselves from them unless a catastrophe befalls us.

Brahim's faithful devotion makes me want to cry; he makes no attempt to flirt with Catherine. To show how much he loves me or in the spirit of sacrifice? How depressing to think he'll stay with me to the end of our days. We are bonded together, broken, damaged, irreparable.

The ruins of Tipasa, nostalgia. The sea makes me feel fragile, I'm physically drained from swimming, from the unexpected appearance of Catherine, from Bruce's strangeness (I can't get used to it). My family is reduced to the status of victim: three timid, neurotic individuals, devoid of ambition. Perhaps it's not loyalty, perhaps Brahim knows he doesn't stand a chance. What kind of man is the actress-mother's husband? The girl-boy's father? I imagine him as the opposite of Brahim, absent (he's gone abroad), charming, fickle, elusive.

I draw a triangle in my notebook to represent the Bousba family, a circle for the Aklis. We are so different.

Women are more of a mystery than men. I have chosen Catherine. Desire and reality distort. What chance do I have?

Little flowers grow in the sand, beyond the confines of the forest that sends tree roots snaking underground like vast arms all the way to the sea, miniature sunflowers among the seaweed, worms, fragments of shells, pieces of nets washed up on the shore by the waves. Nothing is stronger than life, I could blossom in another skin, flourish in other flesh.

Bruce and Erwan come back. I won't tell them I was worried, it would play into the creature's hands. She pushes him as soon as they reach the shore, my son stumbles, gets up without protesting, I let them get on with it, I see it as an initiation rite, a way of defining their roles. My son has a small scratch on his right side, he's no longer mine.

I am writing the whole truth of our story, I swear it, hand on heart.

A snapshot. Bruce standing with the paddle planted in the sand, Erwan, arms folded, perfectly aligned with his friend's immaculate body. The sea is dark in the background, the sky pale, the two figures are sprinkled with light.

Bruce fills the frame of the Polaroid, Erwan, shot from the same angle, is a blur beside her; the lens has captured my son's dismay at falling, at what is happening to us.

Bruce, the lion cub, the classical figurine, Erwan, the fawn, flesh and blood, one child being devoured by another. Catherine emerges from the forest, clutching an armful of heather to her chest: 'For you, Michèle.' I am both bride and victim, beloved and servant; the dry mauve stems feel prickly against my skin. Catherine has let her hair down, I stare at her lips, the fine lines around them, I imagine biting them to avenge my son.

Our four bodies at the centre of the cove, two adults, two children, a magnetic halo around us; Brahim is outside the halo, excluded, looking as if the blood had been drained from his body, searching for a place to conceal his agony. Evening comes to his rescue, we have to leave before dark; we gather up our things in silence, each of us locked in a secret monologue, issuing a challenge to the others.

Catherine and Bruce walk ahead, in thrall to the forest. They walk arm in arm without stopping to wait for us, two lovers enamoured by adventure. Bruce is wearing a white tank top over her swimsuit. She reminds me of a wild child found in a cave, brought up by animals, that's where her survival instinct comes from – a rare intelligence, she's sharp, quick, logical, pitiless, other people are either her enemy or her prey. Catherine's perfume opens a second pathway, superimposed onto the first, light and airy, carrying me towards my imaginings. When will I see her again?

A cross chalked on our gate at home, we erase it, leaving no trace of its existence. There are no signs of any intruders in the garden, no footprints, no sign of a break-in, the garage is securely locked. I can hear the phone ring inside the house, no one picks it up, the sun has left us light-headed: neither Brahim nor I mentions Catherine Bousba and her daughter. We pretend nothing is wrong, act as if this were a trivial encounter, not one with the potential to disrupt the course of our lives, of time itself. Things unspoken cannot exist.

Sheets of dark, slimy seaweed cover the soil in our garden, colonising it, leaving the earth iodised, salty – a poultice that renders the soil more fertile, resilient, its colour changed. The garden seems to ripple, like seaweed billowing in the depths, neutralising the acids in the water.

Peaches that peel easily, offering no resistance to the small Opinel knife cutting into them; I give the tender morsels of flesh to my son to cool him down. The sun has given him a slight fever but he doesn't complain. In his bed, with no dinner, he is filled with the memory of Bruce, of being in the canoe, rowing across the circular waters of the inlet. He calls it the 'circus' – a simple mistake or a symbolic reference to the spectacle that took place there?

Sitting on the steps to the terrace, smoking, feeling tempted to have a drink, wanting at the same time to remain in the 'reality' of Catherine Bousba and not lose sight of it in a haze of alcohol. I want to inhale her perfume exactly as it was, look into the real blue-orange of her eyes, hear her voice without inventing sounds and words. I want to stay faithful to the first glimpse, the dread and wonder of that dazzling vision as I emerged from the water, like the mirage on the road to Tipasa – a precious, volcanic stone. I want to inhabit my desires, urges, loathing, without being forced to choose between falling and being in control.

Bruce's overly large teeth, her husky voice.

The gold watch chain bracelet on Catherine's wrist.

The Bousba family's social class, the wealth and power that go with it.

Bruce's precise choice of words – poetry or the way she's been brought up?

Bruce's father, whose name is never mentioned.

The man's shirt, the wife wearing her absent husband's clothes, a sign of their sensuality, their eroticism.

My clumsy movements (embarrassment) as if my body were suspended from a wire that activates its mechanism.

Brahim – I should have put my arm around him, to establish the rules of the game.

I dig, till the soil, make a hole at the foot of the small tree from Bou Saada, bury Catherine's heather in the earth, hoping to watch it grow beneath the palm trees, a witness to my feelings – I who have no one to confide in. I feel more intensely alone since the day at the beach, destined for secrecy. I miss the desert, we'll be there for Christmas, I'm afraid I'll die (an inner death) before then.

Faïrouz on the record player, singing my favourite track, 'Habaytek Bisayf'. I don't know whether Brahim wants to draw me back to him or hand me over to Catherine. He looks over at me from the living room, I smile at the words of the song that used to be ours:

'I loved you in winter, I loved you in summer. I longed for you in winter, I longed for you in summer. Your eyes are the summer, mine are the winter. We shall meet again, my love, beyond winter and summer.'

I want to throw my notebooks on the fire, purge them.

Summer is over.

The Algeria of my childhood dreams was mysterious, oriental, a land of palaces, dunes, princes, thoroughbred horses, gardens of Eden, verdant moorlands, a country peopled with saints and nymphs dissolving in a haze of steam from hammams, a place of fairy tales and pagan legends. Algeria was waiting for me, I was certain of it, waiting to make me anew. Brahim was the man I'd dreamt of, freeing me of my sorrows, my extreme tendencies (my obsessions); we fell in love and I drew from his strength, I ruled over my house, our son's heart, I ventured into town alone, I walked, solitary and fatalistic among the crowd, I plunged into the belly of the city – Algiers, feminine and Medusa-like despite the dense mass of men. Everything here leads back to the obsession with the body, with desire, with desire fulfilled and desire frustrated.

Love, domestic, everyday, leads me towards death, I'm not normal, I accept it. My life is somewhere in front of me, as if I've missed the turning, taken the wrong road, I'm stuck, going nowhere; if disaster were to strike I'd be paralysed, riveted to the spot amid the chaos, the last to flee the scene.

At what age can you be sure you've missed out on your life, missed out on love? The years ahead should be years of reparation, consolation, but not for me, I shall continue to be swept along by the fate of this land that has stifled its rage.

When I heard Catherine Bousba say: 'I don't fear anything here,' I thought to myself that she must not be afraid of men, she must seek them out to either seduce or humiliate them. She must have found a way to adapt to Algeria, to its madness – she seems untouched by it.

Fear is an illness, a way of looking at the world that strips it of both joy and hope.

Brahim won't allow himself to mention Bruce's mother, he knows it would unleash a torrent of words, he prefers not to witness the birth of a passion, he avoids the subject. His silence gives us a new bond – we say nothing in a bid to avoid being hurt. As a gesture of respect, I refrain from writing in my journal for a while.

IV

An eye in the sky watches over me, a cyclops scrutinising my every move from above. Boredom and guilt. I plunge back into my journal, setting the seal on my treachery. Forgive me, Brahim.

I drive Erwan to school, hoping to see Catherine. No sign of her, she's vanished into thin air. Erwan climbs the school steps. I wait in the car.

I drive up to the Shell building, park outside near the service station to avoid having to declare my identity at the gate. I sketch the building in my notebook, crescent-shaped, a war bunker.

Chéraga market. Apples, celery, parsley, turnips, pumpkins, I stock up on fruit and vegetables – cooking keeps my mind occupied – and busy myself washing, scraping, cutting as if I were working on Catherine's body, wrapping it, embellishing, moisturising.

Walking through the market between the stalls, the smell

of men who live in the countryside, their hands gnarled from working the earth, faces aged by toil and sun. Their smiles remind me of the resistance fighters whose images I found among Brahim's things – cousins, rebels, strangers photographed in their shelters. Women's feet bare in their plastic sandals, slender ankles, skin dyed with henna. Their wrists adorned with golden bangles, ten, twenty sometimes, their bridal dowry. I lose myself in the market, in my thoughts, no one pays any attention to me, no one notices me, I'm just another mother.

A dog on a length of rope beside a man with a glass of milk, a beggar or a dog-trainer.

The crowd. All these hands could reach out and touch me, I'd succumb, I wouldn't fight back. I imagine Bruce bullying Erwan, poking him with her compass, tripping him up in the playground, making him jump from the top of the high bars.

Stocks of chocolate, fromage blanc, tomato concentrate, flour, packets of sugar, semolina, here in this country suffering from shortages. The revolution will come from the poor, the militias promise victory to those who fought and won the war.

Militias, political or religious.

If I'd written in my notebooks during the Algerian War, I'd have kept count of the dead, I'd still be counting the dead with my words, now and in the future. My notebook would be written in red ink. I have a premonition of war, a war that no one is expecting.

Algeria, a young country, spoken of like a young man whose delicate beauty is still unfolding.

What kind of lives do they lead, these men and women of the market? Catherine is right, we don't have enough time to decipher everyone's heart. So many lives to be lived, so many missed opportunities.

I could go and meet Brahim at the factory, surprise him, fling my arms around him, kiss him in front of his employees. I go the opposite way, back to the centre of town and up towards the Shell building. I park just beneath it and a soldier asks me to move on for reasons of security — the French Embassy is next door.

I drive around, hoping to come upon the elusive woman who has disappeared from view — intentionally, or is she simply indifferent? I am of no importance. Time casts a mantle over our days, the day at the beach is a fading memory.

I don't know what goes on in the evening in the Shell building.

People say a woman walks through the grounds whistling the tune to 'Min Jibalina', the anthem of the patriots.

The foundations are unstable, the wind blows continuously.

Residents have found swords and champagne glasses hidden in a false ceiling, wrapped in newspaper.

A water tank containing dollars, Deutschmarks, francs, hard currency as they say here.

A homeless person sleeps in the tall grass between the walls of a ruined structure that the local residents say will one day become a mosque.

The building has its own legends, I shall invent one for Bruce and Catherine.

Cool evenings, the sky heavy with clouds, ships passing from port to port, carrying messages to Europe. Alone in the kitchen I slice into the leg of lamb and infuse the flesh with garlic, sprigs of thyme and rosemary – as if I were inflicting torture, taking revenge for my solitude, my long days, my uncertain future.

Red wine, warm, heavy. Then some gardening, everyday gestures, setting the garden in order before the frosts, preparing for the winter season – just as I make myself ready for sex.

Brahim has placed pieces of broken glass on top of the main façade of our house, the one that faces the street, 'as a precaution'. I don't feel any threat here, I am as adept with knives as I am with betrayal.

The lamb sizzles in the oven, overflowing with juices and blood, the outside grilling, a carapace protecting the tender parts within.

Erwan in his pyjamas in front of the television watching *The Protectors*, Brahim on the sofa, the perfect family, each of us going about our business, relaxing.

Brahim: 'Never mention politics to anyone. Don't ever say the president's name on the phone.'

Lack of tenderness can make you paranoid.

The words of the theme song to Erwan's show: 'The avenues and alleyways, where the soul of a man is easy to buy, everybody's wheeling, everybody's dealing.'

The balance of my mind is in sync with the balance of the country. I let the wine wash over me, one glass is enough for me to become airborne without anyone noticing.

I think of the city opening up to the night, to women whose lives men have shattered. I wonder how Catherine spends her nights, I imagine her lurking in the port, courting danger, with Bruce on a leash to avoid losing her, like the beggar and his dog in the market.

She commands men's respect, she is the one who decides. I must see her again, learn from her.

Catherine has allowed Bruce's nature to flourish, her place as the only woman in the family is undisturbed.

In Brahim's arms, I play the child, falling asleep bathed in his perfume of soap and eau de Cologne. He is not my father but he is still Erwan's, when I allow him to be.

The phone rings, waking me from my sleep, and then falls silent. In my dream the garden has pulled back, climbed up towards the Shell building to cover its façade with brambles, thorns and mosses.

Long skirt, heels, ivory blouse, beige jacket, a brooch. I put on some eye make-up, lipstick, a dab of perfume on the inside of both elbows, the back of the knees, behind the ears – tempting fate.

Before going to get Erwan, I make some mille-feuilles by soaking biscuits in coffee and chilling them in the refrigerator for several hours. When they've set, I'll cut them into four or six pieces.

The landscape around me seems both familiar and strange. I gaze at our bedroom, our garden, our house, my instincts telling me that when I come back I'll have changed, that something is going to happen.

Autumn and summer merging, Algeria's climate. I whistle the tune of the patriots' song, like the phantom woman who haunts the Shell building.

Men at war. Ancient Tipasa, Palestro, the Battle of Algiers. And tomorrow? Ensnared by the city, I am imprisoned in my house, waiting for my executioners. I will not forsake Algeria, my final homeland, my country, my youth. I, the Frenchwoman, the object of no one's gaze.

My adoration of this land has spilt over into my garden, its flowers and trees have taught me to be patient.

Brahim kisses me when he leaves for the factory as if he is never coming back, as if he has understood everything. My life is a dream. I'm not in love with Catherine. What I want is to touch the nerve of life.

When I was young, I was fascinated by death – it rose up like a promised land, offering the possibility of escape, of flight. Now life has become like that mysterious land. Days have followed one after another, leading nowhere, severing love from desire.

Catherine is the crowning glory of my madness. And then I become aware of my ravings and I'm ashamed.

I have no knowledge of women's bodies. I don't know what a female body can offer another woman, what it can represent for her. I don't know if this desire is real, if it exists on its own, free of attachments or if it is linked to someone else – a man, orchestrating the scene for his own pleasure.

My view of women is wrong. I spend too much time in the kitchen. I must go out to work, I must broach the subject of the French lycée again with Brahim.

My role as mother, housewife and, at the opposite extreme, my fantasies of torture chambers, pleasures of the damned. Two worlds: my home and the abyss. The gulf between them is too great.

My son, wearing a sweatshirt and jacket. I imagine Bruce dressed for autumn, proudly aware of her image, capable of standing up for herself in the face of taunts. I know how strong she is: Erwan is still wearing his sheriff badge. My thoughts leapfrog from her to Catherine, the ambush I'm planning – using our children's friendship to draw her closer, inviting Bruce to our house to lure Catherine here. She won't come.

In my imagination I am her plaything. A vision I loathe and adore in equal measure.

I give Erwan a hug before we get in the car to go to school. I worry that my obsession with the Bousbas, this family I know nothing about, is preventing me from giving my own child enough love and attention.

Madame Ziad, our neighbour, tells me a man tried to force open the door to our garage – he ran away when he realised she was watching him. No break-in. 'He won't come back,' I say to reassure her, 'just a thief who happened to be passing by.' I won't mention it to Brahim. I think we pay too much attention to our fears – we should pack them away in boxes. Desire restores balance. I am innocent, for now.

The skies are empty, birds have fled, flights have been cancelled, clouds of insects dispersed; no dust, no fallen leaves. I drive down to the Hydra school, Elton John playing on the car stereo, 'Song for Guy'. I'm all alone, abandoning my son, guided by intuition, a forest of roses, a crystal fountain.

Catherine is outside the school with Bruce. They're arguing about something. She has her arm around Bruce's shoulders.

If I were to take a picture, the image would show the concrete of the building, Catherine's red nail polish and Bruce's felt peaked cap.

Erwan gets out of the car, runs over to Bruce, Catherine lets go of her daughter, a process of transferral, me delivering my son, Catherine advancing towards me, two actions flowing smoothly into one another. I am swapping my life for another, exchanging maternal attachment for a state of bewitchment.

She doesn't have the car this morning, they walked down. I offer to give her a lift; she asks if I know the Shell building.

Our children climb the steps and disappear into the world of schoolchildren, I am stepping into a forbidden life.

I start the car, hands shaking as I clutch the steering wheel, all but swooning as I smell that perfume from the day at the beach again. I feel as if I'm floating inside my skin, it's too big for me, like my clothes. I could go and sit in the back seat, let Bruce's mother drive me, mother and son on the road through the reeds.

Catherine is dressed in jeans, sandals, an off-the-shoulder top – a calculated look, she's thought it all out. I could call Brahim for help, but he too has ceased to exist.

Algiers, a new city.

My lilac, my birds of paradise, my jasmine, my medlar tree, my palm tree from Bou Saada, the soil in my garden, a faithless woman's earth.

Bruce is being difficult, she says. She doesn't want to go to school. I don't realise how lucky I am with Erwan. I don't answer. She knows nothing about us, I don't want her to know anything. Things mutate when taken out of context. Catherine is razor-sharp.

The scent of her breath on the air. She's not carrying a bag, only a key ring, a pack of cigarettes, her lighter.

Bruce, in a jacket to match her corduroy trousers, a boy-girl sulking, not crying.

Catherine offers me a cigarette, we roll down the windows and smoke, a shared intimacy, our first. The children in the street seem to be laughing at me. Catherine's body in my car is a double of the body at the beach. I'm not sure I can believe it.

The Shell building. The man at the gate hands Catherine her mail. What if he recognises me as the madwoman? A ramp runs alongside the buildings – the solid mass of the structures seems more imposing when viewed from the inside. Covered terraces, blocks of flats standing on concrete pilings, the upper floors reaching to touch the sky. No light penetrates here, no signs of plant life, nothing but the eucalyptus forest that surrounds the French Embassy next door.

I miss my house, my sheets – a shroud for our marriage. I might never go back to Brahim. I might be swept away by a mirage.

Parking spaces covered by a concrete awning. I park in Bruce's father's spot. His name is Amar.

Amar, his existence in the space between us.

My skirt is wrinkled, I feel embarrassed. Catherine walks around to my side, offers me her hand as I get out of the car, playing the man to my woman. I hate this scene. Electric cables run from the entrance to the courtyard, linking their phone lines to ours. I follow her, she could be taking me down to the basement to tie me up and leave me there, forgotten.

Men, their physical appearance, their smell, their strength, their voice, the way they walk, smoke, kiss. How they are in moments of ecstasy and at rest. I know nothing of women, I have so little knowledge of myself. A memory of ballerinas, spinning, separating. For me, there is no union between women. If Bruce were to desire Erwan, what kind of love would my son be involved in? The Bousba family is in command, we are their subjects.

They live on the top floor, we have to take the lift, a box that slides up and down a wall in front of the landings. I expect Brahim has tried phoning me, he'll be worried. I'm out on the edge of our world.

Catherine's hair is like seaweed in the garden, it will sap the essence of my being, its salts and sugars. The feeling that other people will always be better than I am: Bruce, Catherine, the beggar with the dog in the market.

I step over the threshold of the apartment in this building at the top of the hill in Hydra, the futuristic structure that is Bruce's home. This is where she has grown up, in her concrete tower. A space built to satisfy material needs, a link between inner and outer worlds, a passageway for boredom and violence. To one side, the Mitidja plain, to the other, the sea, out of reach.

I search for signs of Bruce's father, Amar – a desk, files on the shelves, photos, a stack of records, books of poetry. He's an oilman, representing Algeria abroad, defending its interests, negotiating for his country.

Her husband has chosen his country over her, she has been replaced.

They met in Paris, at a party; it all happened very quickly. She's impulsive. Algeria wasn't a dream destination for her, it's an experience like any other. She and her husband each have their own lives, they don't discuss them, they come together when he returns from his travels. They slip back into their daily routines, the two of them, the three of them with Bruce, whom her father finds difficult, alarming. He lacks patience.

Michèle.

Her voice speaking my name.

Their married life is a series of interruptions, she says, it swings back and forth between fulfilment and absence. I can see the study from the living room, both rooms open out onto a terrace, there's a hallway separating the bedrooms from the living area. I imagine Bruce running through the flat, creating havoc, challenging her father. Algiers is invisible from here, the eucalyptus forest forms a barrier, the building is isolated, its secrets well-guarded.

Brahim.

Her voice speaking his name.

I tell her how Brahim and I met. I talk about university, idealism, my son, my love for him, our house, this country, my aversion to it. About how I don't feel liked by the inhabitants, how I'm in awe of nature, held captive by it. I keep my melancholy (my illness) in check, I don't want to lose control of it. I say nothing about my lack of desire for the man who stole my youth. I picture Brahim with Catherine, the image of one superimposed on the other.

She finds him attractive.

A slap in the face among women who love men.

Her apartment, where she lives, loves, hates, kisses, climaxes, goes to sleep. I could write so much about Catherine, real and unreal. I can't picture her cooking, washing, tidying, she is the spirit of the place, not the servile wife, an acquisition.

The terrace is circular, the tiles, terracotta. Catherine points to a white roof surrounded by overgrown vegetation, our house. I imagine Bruce with a telescope, watching us, phoning us, disturbing our peace.

The gardens are set back from the building, trees growing beyond the confines of the stone and concrete structures, almond, lemon and orange trees, their branches reaching towards the forest that surrounds the French Embassy – plant intelligence, the innate order of organic matter.

The parents' bedroom. Mirror, dressing table, jewellery, a stack of *Playboy* magazines, a blue chair with a dress thrown over it. On the bedside table, an ashtray, a book, *The Hite Report*.

A French window leads onto a terrace screened by a line of reeds, protected from view even at this height, so high I feel as if I am paying a visit to the clouds and the sky. A blow-up mattress, a lounger. I catch a glimpse of a bathroom and recognise the smell of her perfume.

The sense of a man's presence, even though Amar is away.

The bed is made, sheets pulled taut, pillowcases smooth. My eyes are microscopes, taking it all in, committing it to memory. My brain will develop the images registered by my gaze, fixing them like photographic compositions.

On to Bruce's room. I'm one step ahead of my son, stealing his friendship, inspecting the place where he'll soon be coming to play and sleep. Walls plastered with Bruce Lee posters, tacked on, overlapping, glued together, ripped, repaired with Sellotape, images of Bruce Lee in flight, leaping through the air, reproduced to infinity.

The bedroom is a scene of struggles, battles fought by the film star Kung Fu master, by Catherine's daughter as she absorbs the blood of her icon.

Male violence has drawn her out of her femininity. This is where her battle is waged, fed by the power of her god with his strange and celebrated beauty. He is responsible for her transgression, for the physique she has built despite her natural slenderness.

A pair of boxing gloves, nunchucks hanging on a hook, her bedroom a cell for both torture and reflection. Writing pads on a desk, their pages covered with words I can't read written in Bruce's hand. I imagine them to be hypnotic chants, profane hymns, embellished with criss-crossing lines, her ink drawings symbolising infinity and imprisonment.

On her bedside table, a framed snapshot of Bruce Lee in a dinner jacket against a backdrop of Californian palm trees. Near the frame, a map of the cove and the Polaroid image of Bruce standing with the paddle, my son a blur.

I miss Erwan, I find it hard to imagine him asleep beneath the posters but I know it's too late, we'll come back here. My delicate boy can provide the feminine side that's missing in Bruce. Their relationship is a fusion, an experiment.

I see myself as a serial killer, and yet I am the one in the lion's mouth. The Shell building is my new Eldorado.

The phone rings. Catherine leaves it unanswered.

Bruce writes. She's like me, we're made of the same stuff, stone that is hard to crack.

Amar is probably rough, impatient. A man's trench coat hangs in the hallway. Another mirror where Catherine must have adjusted her sweater to offer me her shoulder, her collar bone, the swell of a breast. I can't help thinking how proud an Algerian man must be with a French woman standing at his side. A racist thought.

Bruce's bedroom, a den of sadomasochism.

I take off my cardigan. Thousands of blood vessels radiate beneath my blouse, like the branches of trees, shimmering, alert. A vision of Brahim at the factory surrounded by rolls of the very paper I use to write of our demise. Little does he know.

We have coffee in the kitchen, ceramic worktops, laundry room at the back with washing on the line – now I understand the reason for the slits in the walls that make me think of firing posts and machine guns. She hates this place, she'd rather have her own house.

Amar is often away, at least they're safe here. I imagine Catherine in my garden, the sun's rays hitting her as they filter through the foliage.

Amar is too protective. She's not afraid at all, she sees nothing to be frightened of here. She is full of admiration for this country. She's lying, testing me. Her blue eyes flecked with orange, I could stretch out my arm, draw her skin close to mine, that's all it would take to trigger the countdown for the nuclear explosion. The wind has changed, it will take control of the sea, capsize the fragile crafts. The Mediterranean Sea, a graveyard.

The doorbell rings.

She excuses herself, goes to answer it.

I inspect her refrigerator while she's out of the room. A fish wrapped in newspaper, a fin sticking out. I'm ashamed of myself: 'Who are you, Michèle Akli?'

I wait.

Voices, a man's, then Catherine's, asking him not to try and see her again.

She comes back. I can't stay, I have to leave, escape into

the vortex of my words, suspend myself from the creepers in my garden. I'm out of place here.

My jacket, my bag, I gather up my things.

I take the stairs down, the lift terrifies me. Outside, the concrete pillars echo the columns in the apartment. I have visions of Catherine suspended from a beam by a belt, Bruce being punished for the sin of being the way she is.

I take the ramp towards the exit, the gatekeeper raises the barrier, our house is just down the road, I only have to drive past the service station, a few hundred metres, and I'm back in our garage. Inside that apartment I felt a million miles away from my world, no longer in Algeria; it wasn't me, it wasn't Brahim, it never will be.

I feel as though Catherine's body is inside mine, I have her hair, her eyes, her voice — a sensation of being possessed. Dark images of the gardens around the residence, the devil's garden. Only writing can bring me back to reality.

Bruce has stolen the snapshot taken at the beach. Or maybe Erwan gave it to her as a gift, a souvenir, a way of repaying the debt of the sheriff's badge.

The submissive gene.

The man at the door could be a singing teacher, a lover, the driver of the black CX who never gets out of the car.

I call Brahim at the factory, ask him to pick Erwan up from

school. I pretend I'm not feeling well and reassure him, as I must, his wife is a fragile creature; I hate being condemned to this. I hate Brahim. I need my garden, my trees, their bark, my terrace steps, wine. It's too early for wine, mixing alcohol and Catherine would be madness.

Cornflowers, hyacinths, hydrangeas – the flowers of my childhood – before Algeria with its succulents – barbary fig, agave, cactus, aloe – oozing, sweating, spilling over with sap, fecund and full of seed.

Land of contrasts, explosions of relief born of frustration.

The sun is both builder and destroyer, from dawn's first light we crave its power, the pain it brings, night is merely an interlude, the sun will always draw us back. Living to the south of the European continent, on the edge of the desert, creates confusion.

My desire is held in check, directed towards neither Brahim nor Catherine. If she had given me a sign I would have made a move, kissed her, ready to be reborn from my ashes. I have never looked at women like this, never seen them in terms of physical possession. I must open a new chamber in my brain, somewhere to place her pack of cigarettes, the dimple in her left cheek when she smiles, her torso, her breasts and buttocks, a room both romantic and pornographic that I would be able to visit without fear of being compromised.

The day is long, it's early, I must fill the hours, embrace Brahim, the husband I've betrayed. My loathing is as strong as the affection I feel. I picture Catherine in her apartment, she washes my coffee cup, licks the rim, throws it into the rubbish bin, disgusted. The building is retreating towards the Mitidja plain, a ship driven off course by the wind, visible from the moon. Monuments built by men for glory, for satellites.

The turmoil of desiring and not desiring. I censor myself, obey my own commands; I'm not like Bruce. She'll lead my son towards the swamp of shame; Erwan will steer her back to the right path. Bruce is like Catherine, mother and daughter are seducers of innocent souls. Amar has no place with them, he is a world-traveller, he exists by his absence. His returns are brief celebrations, then he disappears again, excluded from the passion of the couple his presence disturbs. Motherhood is a marriage to which men are not invited. They find refuge in other arms, other mothers for whom they are the chosen ones, the favoured sons.

A brief hiatus, I have a few hours left before Erwan and Brahim come home, enough time for me to quell my obsession with Catherine. I won't mention the apartment, the grounds, the stairs, the fear that consumed me as I climbed them, imagining the man at the door hiding in the lift, armed with a knife, ready to leap out at me, confusing me with her, and slitting my throat.

The sounds of the Shell building in my ears as I draw a plan of the residence in my notebook, the stone steps, the ruined annex, the covered walkways, the apartment, terraces, the columns, Bruce's room – images of rituals, macabre rites.

Rosemary's Baby.

Mother and daughter don't look at all alike. What if Catherine had adopted Bruce and brought her up like this as an experiment, forced her to be masculine and to become the ideal companion, the submissive lover, the lifelong chosen one?

An evil spell, I'm sure of it.

Poppy fields, a snapshot.

I used to take Erwan out to the country when he was little. We'd walk through cedar forests and cornfields, roll around on carpets of daisies, climb orange trees. I taught him where clouds came from, how different plants tasted, the pleasures of tree-hugging.

Erwan loved me unconditionally. I was his queen. But the kingdom he thought he knew so well was already crumbling. I taught him about his father's country, we need to know where we come from if we are ever to understand and be close to other people.

I embarked on a second life in a country I loved, but my love for it waned with my fading admiration for Brahim. For me there was both an outer and an inner Algeria. It existed on the outside at the edge of the forest, at the gates of the desert and on the seashore. But inside me, it was on my skin, in my flesh and in my husband's breath.

My desire crumbled to dust in the whirlwind of routines and disappointed hopes, a swirl of pollen, ashes and dust. I have lost. My son will leave me: we need heroes around us to learn.

V

In town. A stream of cars, of men and women, entrails, hollows. The capital city is overcrowded, dense, frantic, frightening – the antithesis of nature. A labyrinth of violence that I fear but cannot give up. I have left my stamp on it; if I were to perish, my garden is where I would lie, but I would leave a small fragment of myself ground into the stone and beaten earth of Algiers's buildings and balconies, in the skies above the city.

I order a lamb shoulder from the butcher on the Rue d'Isly to make Erwan some chorba, a thick soup of tomatoes, meat, coriander and vermicelli. I bury Catherine and her apartment beneath a mountain of tasks.

Once a French cook, now an Algerian cook.

We are the people we cook for; Erwan's dual heritage is becoming less apparent, he is growing up, taking on his father's mannerisms, copying him.

The garden is changing – vines, moss and bushes cover the flowers, protecting them. The days are shorter, Brahim comes home later, I don't ask why. He says nothing as I get up to check the garage doors, turn off the lights in the garden, the appliances, the gas. I've outsmarted Bruce, she won't steal Erwan away from me, I have pilfered scraps of her soul, her Bruce Lee posters, her handwriting.

The snapshot I took will continue the transformation, blurring the contours of her silhouette to reveal the outlines of my son, in the flesh, prepared to do battle with his feelings.

I suggest to Erwan that he invites his friend over, hoping that here, under my own roof, I'll be able to tame her and take control of my savage desire for her mother.

Am I the one manipulating or am I the victim of my own lies?

10cc on the radio, singing 'I'm not in love'.

Trips in the car, like the journeys my heart takes – there was a point of departure, there will be an arrival. Pointe Pescade or the shops at the foot of Catherine Bousba's residence? Which route will open the doors to the forbidden city? I think I see her in the traffic, in the CX, with an older man.

My imagination runs riot where she is concerned.

She is stern, unfaithful, cruel, seductive.

Her movements are precise, her enunciation clear, she wears her clothes like skin, her skin like clothes.

Her polished fingernails, toenails.

She wears her hair up, she bites her lip.

She is a lover, a wife. I don't see her as a mother.

Her childhood is a blank.

She is the first woman, the woman for all women, at the top of the pyramid, the embodiment of femininity, she radiates an ease, a carnal lust I imagine men find desirable in my stunted, remote, neurotic world.

She is no easy prey.

She slips away the moment the hunter approaches.

Catherine.

Regret at not having stolen one of her things from the apartment, keeping it with me, in my hand.

Regret at not having kept her cigarette butt in the ashtray in my car.

Regret at not having warned her about Bruce and Erwan.

Love's contradictions. My heart is enslaved.

Mine are the sailors, thieves, scoundrels, hers are the emperors, the young scions.

She is the one who walks away, not the one who is left.

She is indifferent to love, to sentimentality.

She is the subject of every song I hear. I am ashamed.

Vermicelli, angel hair, a child's treat after school.

Erwan's drawings — tanks, planes, men in uniform, castles, horses — will never intersect with Bruce's drawings.

Sitting on my son's bed, safe in his room, I watch him doing his homework, bending over his notebook as if trying to see his face reflected in water. Childhood is a world of imaginings that must not be shattered. Bruce has no child-hood, her future is stunted.

If Catherine were to set her sights on Brahim, if they were seeing each other behind my back, kissing and speaking ill of me in their secret meetings, I would simply have to wait. Brahim would not be able to sustain the affair, she would say thank you to him and he'd come crying back to me.

My husband's beauty is not sexual. I dream of him being tormented and abused, he submits.

When we danced together, I felt protected for ever. Over the years I've dreamt of him leaving me, of fighting to bring him back to me and seducing him. Peace of mind is the graveyard of desire. Lust is a flame that must be fanned.

In our chaste sleep, Brahim lies pressed to my hip, either to stop himself falling or to reassure me. My only fear at the moment is Catherine. Brahim is content with the tenderness I've started to show him again. He kisses me on the forehead.

I dream of a band of women armed with bows and arrows, characters from prehistoric paintings in Tassili, I am the prisoner in their midst, the victim to be tortured and sacrificed. Catherine arouses primitive passions in me, the physical craving I felt when I was first awakened to sexual ecstasy and left stunned, impatient for more.

I am trapped in the madness of desire. Mist blankets the earth, a fog of souls dragged along in our wake, unable to fly free, tragic, damned. I'm becoming like them.

My ashes will be scattered in my garden one day.

I am both mother and woman, two bodies in opposition. Erwan suspects nothing – the bliss of ignorance.

Lemon meringue pie: beat the eggs, melt the butter, stir in the sugar, cut the fruit in half, squeeze out the juice, sift the flour, flatten the pastry with a fist, roll it out, put it in the oven, wait, watch, manageable gestures, performed again and again by a body in need of care, healing.

The sickness of love.

Bruce is at the gate; she rang the bell, she's waiting. I stay in the kitchen, send Erwan to let her in. She comes in holding a bunch of flowers picked from the gardens of the residence. She's come on her own, on foot, without Catherine. She walks towards me to greet me, I don't offer my cheek. She's wearing a parka, polo-neck top, trousers, combat boots, dressed like a soldier, either to intimidate Erwan, to bring him to heel in his own house, or to send me a warning: stay away from my mother.

Orange juice and biscuits while the pie cooks, Bruce isn't hungry, thank you. No soft edges in her startled gaze.

Her eyes animal-like, she looks lost.

She's cut her hair – Bruce Lee-style.

She takes off her parka, places it on the sofa, I leave it there, afraid to touch it. I watch her move about the house, walking through the living room, out onto the terrace, up the stairs.

The face and body of a boy, I try, and fail, to see the girl in her; Bruce – is she an aberration or a miracle of nature?

What if we were all double creatures, if society was mistaken in assigning us to one gender? What if Bruce was right?

I'm hurt by my son's admiration for Bruce, I'm not jealous, just sad for Erwan, something is missing for him, he knows it; he follows her, pleading, she's his idol. Her idol is Bruce Lee. My son is no one's idol.

They are ten years old.

So young and already they see authority as a symbol of desire, with roles assigned, tension.

Bruce is not Erwan's killer, it's herself she's assassinating, she's murdering the girl-child to allow the boy to flourish; her drawings and writings tell the story of her suicide.

Nature must be obeyed, we cannot betray our birthright and walk against the tide of humanity. I've stopped admiring her, I feel sorry for her. She suffers in silence. To weep over her fate would be to admit her crime.

She's changed her name in a bid to alter her fate.

I don't sense any affection towards Erwan from her – she's using him, he's a distraction for her, she dominates him. She sees herself as superior to real boys, he makes her feel at ease in her distorted image of herself.

She's clever. Bruce, the sage.

I never wanted a second child, I didn't want to risk having a girl, I wouldn't have known how to bring her up, I'd have been jealous of her relationship with Brahim, with Erwan. I'm the only woman in my household, the mirror image of Catherine. Women don't like other women.

Catherine hasn't called to check that Bruce has arrived safely; does she have our phone number?

There's no solidarity among women. The empire of men may have destroyed the empire of women.

My desire for Catherine springs from jealousy. I don't long to kiss her, I want to revel in her strength, her freedom. She is my own personal pin-up.

Love is fleeting, Erwan will come to his senses, I will too.

Bruce's posy of violets, dandelions, autumn crocuses, grasses, tightly wrapped in a sheath of weeds. I wonder if Catherine put them together or if Bruce spent time choosing the flowers to give me; I have a fleeting, but false, image of Bruce harbouring some emotion towards me, an image soon dispelled when I see the way she looks at my attire. I'm sitting on the steps, they don't want me bothering them, I go back to my kitchen, my pie has risen, like my heart that is swollen with my tears.

Shouts, laughter, Bruce's untamed nature unleashed in the garden, a wild animal capable of destroying, demolishing, laying waste to my plants, my flowers, my trees as well as my son. I have great faith in Erwan, he's in her hands but he is vigilant, perhaps she'll share some of her powers with my innocent son.

Brahim is fading into the background, like the memory of the day at the beach; he's left the house and gone into town to get away from the children, from me too perhaps. Our bodies no longer come together at night.

Our marriage is devoid of desire. Our silence about this is suffocating me — we say nothing to stop it from existing, coming back at us, springing a surprise. Maybe Catherine can be of help to us.

I find the thought of Erwan 'playing the girl' intolerable, an attitude that reveals my latent misogyny. I hate myself.

I leave the kitchen and see Erwan and Bruce in the fig tree, sitting on the highest branch. The vision of our bodies, hanging, comes back to me, joined now by Catherine's and her daughter's too.

Yesterday Brahim said that a man came to the factory and asked him if he was supplying paper to the French Embassy and the Algerian press. The man checked all the records of orders and deliveries.

Catherine is a shield. Together we hurl insults at the militia, fight off the thief in the garage, punch the driver of the Renault 8. I become a man in her company. Women's weakness, men despising them for it. Brahim's gentleness does nothing to reassure me. He wouldn't be able to defend us, he'd be the first to die, he wouldn't even be witness to our suffering.

I picture Catherine on the terrace of her apartment, watching her daughter and my son as they play, trying to locate me, the figure appearing and disappearing in their play area. They're growing, getting older, like the roots beneath their feet spreading their unseen tentacles, cracking the foundations of the house and the neighbouring buildings, threading their way down towards the town, searching for a place to find purchase on the seabed.

I don't know whether Amar has come back, Bruce doesn't mention her parents, she's ashamed of them, or maybe she's protecting them – she's trying to work out what I'm up to, guessing at what my intentions are, misinterpreting them.

I want Catherine, but only in my fantasies, I'd be incapable of acting on them, even if she were to ask me to. Fear condemns me to sensual isolation. It's madness to think she could desire me; with my ill-fitting clothes, my melancholy thoughts, my mood swings, I'm not her type at all, I'm sure she associates with women like herself, women who are free, beautiful, desirable, or women who make their living by giving pleasure and slipping away without a word of farewell.

In reality, I wouldn't know what to do to her; in my imagination I can let myself be led by her desire, obeying her voice, her words, her gestures, following her orders. Our affair would be a second birth. At first I'd be assiduous and compliant, but then I'd learn, gain knowledge and experience and eventually I would bring back the depraved lovers of my imaginings and I'd be punished for my unfaithfulness.

Women's gentleness, a myth.

Bruce and Erwan come in from the garden and go to my son's room. He closes his shutters, something he never does, he's afraid of the dark, he likes to look out at the garden from his room, the shadows of the trees on the walls, the frenetic activity of birds in spring.

I don't intervene. I wait. His room is becoming Bruce's room. She's taken command, just as I imagined she would, she's decided to turn it into a secret game.

My son, my love – I long to go into the room, tear him away from Bruce, grapple with her, slap her. But you can't fight with a child.

Catherine's daughter has the look and mannerisms of someone who has already lived a life in hell: attaching herself to her prey to seek revenge or initiate her victim into violence. Bruce is a force of evil, Erwan is the lamb.

Her strong arms, her biceps, powerful shoulders and muscular torso as she leaps expertly from branch to branch in the garden, humiliating Erwan, the boy.

She belongs in a freak show. I'm ashamed of saying this.

Anyone reading my journals would be forced to change their view of me: my son, astonished to learn of my jealousy, Brahim, reading the story of our love, a castle abandoned to the winds and the crows, Catherine, laughing at me and ripping out the passages about her. Only Bruce would be pleased, thrilled to see that she had been acknowledged.

My words cleanse my soul, soften the pain. Things that are written about exist in a different form, distorting reality, showing it to be broken, outdated, and making it palatable. Bruce could steal my notebooks, make me confess, demand money in exchange or a piece of Erwan's flesh that she would grow in a test tube and graft to her own skin.

Bruce could absorb my notebooks into hers, telling my story, passing as me, possessing me: a form of metempsychosis where one soul is invited to live in another's body.

I don't know if the past can be assimilated into the present. The future unsettles it, of that I am certain. I have dreams of beheadings, of disembowelment, of warring families, of tragedy befalling Algeria. War is being waged under a different name. I must go on writing, hurtling towards the future.

In the garden, posted outside Erwan's tightly shuttered window, I hear music – the Eagles, 'Hotel California' – no voices, no laughter. Are they dancing arm in arm? Or are they sitting cross-legged, playing dice, cards and jacks?

Does Erwan see her as a girl? Or does he think of her as a boy, giving himself permission for a relationship that he finds neither shocking nor alarming? Bruce would be the first boy in Erwan's love life, throwing open the story of his heart, of his life, my son could be 'testing' himself with

Bruce, practising. There would be nothing to stop him from desiring a 'real' boy in the future; Bruce could be preparing him, schooling him in masculine relationships. If anyone were to ridicule him, Erwan wouldn't have to sacrifice his honour – Bruce is still a girl. With adolescence she'll soon become more feminine – unless her willpower proves stronger than nature and Bruce succeeds in stopping her blood flow, constraining her hips, her breasts.

Does Bruce think of Erwan as a boy? Or has she seen a fragility in him, a fragility that is wrongly attributed to girls? She called him The River the day they met, she gave herself the right to comfort him and perhaps to persecute him, to be both saviour and tyrant; her first affair, training herself before conquering the hearts of real women. I doubt it.

Bruce is not in love with Erwan, she's not going to be, she draws out in him the qualities she lacks; Erwan is gentle, but his body is changing, he'll soon be her rival, my son will be stronger than Bruce. It won't be long before the two friends go their separate ways.

What if an only child bears the burden of their parents' unfulfilled fantasies for a child of the opposite sex? What if a boy's body were to grow into a girl's, or a girl's were to grow into a boy's, to compensate for the absence of either a boy or a girl and console the parents' buried sorrows?

We are obsessed by the need to find our spectral selves. We search for our invisible, complementary side, hoping to find it in love. And when we are disappointed, we search again, and lose our way again.

I place my palms on Bruce's handprints in the branches of the fig tree, picture her flying like Bruce Lee from branch to branch without crashing to the ground. What star could have cast a shadow over her birth?

Autumn, season of fading. My flowers seem to have fallen asleep, the leaves go on climbing up the wall, intertwining without damaging each other, resisting the rains and the storms. My body, solitary, unfulfilled, Catherine's ubiquitous presence, a second skin growing beneath my own. I shall be disappointed, as lovers are when they don't see themselves reflected in the gaze of their beloved.

The meringue is perfect, rust-coloured and white, a coating of sullied snow perfectly suspended over the layer of lemon, frothy and spattered with air holes, thick enough to retain its shape, its integrity. I set the table in the kitchen, a mother of two.

I call them. I don't venture into the bedroom.

Bruce has taken off her jumper, an army pullover with a badge roughly stitched on, Erwan has undone two of his shirt buttons, his hair is sweaty, clinging to his forehead, they've been fighting, or perhaps not – Erwan will tell me. He's incapable of lying, just like his father.

The way Bruce glares at me makes me uncomfortable, the furious child raging against adults who can't look at her without examining her, can't speak of her without wondering. Difference is an affront – I think back to what Catherine said about Bruce's father finding her difficult. Bruce is from another time, a creature from the ancient past, half-human, half-animal, a character from a story, from Noah's Ark.

The three of us. Silence brings me closer to their childhood. I become a little girl again, an unpleasant sensation. Further away in town, Brahim drives to get away from us. Higher up the hill, Catherine is pleasuring herself in my imagination, behind her husband's back, behind Bruce's back, between earth and sky, clothed only in her hair.

Bruce.

Her bitten nails.

Her bird-like appetite.

Her fringe cut diagonally, sticking up on top of her head.

Her sweaty smell.

Her legs crossed.

Nervy and slender.

Her beauty has abandoned her.

She wants to go home, refuses my offer of a lift.

Erwan and I watch her from the gate; she rounds the bend and disappears from sight.

I imagine her walking faster, hurrying to get back to her own home, the building made for her, a protective cover for her every move, to her homework exercises, her drawings, her writing, her prayers, her idol, hurrying to get back to her mother and burrow into her supple body, diving into the cradling fluids, mother's milk, blood, warm flesh, oxygen, breathing again, clinging to Catherine's ribs as she clung to the branches in my garden.

Wine brings me back up, I resurface, a deep-sea diver. The back of my son's neck, his smell, his kisses, he is the opposite of Bruce — he is the clearing, she is the forest, he is the sky, she is darkness, he is hope, she is menace.

Changing of the guard. Brahim is back home again, taking Erwan's place. I cup his face in my hands, I love them both, with the same love.

I try to reconstruct Bruce's face in my journal, her features are a blur, I can't see her, nothing can pin her down, hold her in place.

I'm struck by terror that something has happened to her on the way home; I remember what the boys playing football had said about her: '*ataï*', faggot. The line of houses with their overflowing gardens will protect her, absorb her.

Bruce has returned to the earth's magma where she was conceived, her womb.

I don't say anything to Erwan about his bedroom, the music, the closed shutters; I'm afraid of hearing the truth, afraid of upsetting him. Childhood, feathers and down.

I imagine Bruce retracing her steps along our road, walking down towards the city, disappearing into the crowd of men, seeing herself reflected in them, continuing towards the arcades, the docks, the port, climbing aboard a cargo ship, hiding inside a container.

Erwan takes off his shirt for me to wash and I notice a scratch on his belly, 'the rosebush,' he says. Drops of dried blood have formed a perfect line on his skin. Bruce's wound.

I wish I'd insisted on taking her home, I should call, but I don't want to hear Catherine's voice, I'd be troubled by it, my night would be disturbed, my dreams. Boredom has created a bond; I am weaving a cloth of gold thread around the figure of a woman. Our only connection is Algiers, it divides us too. My spitefulness, its stitches the opposite of embroidery. Did I not insist on taking Bruce home because all I wanted was to be rid of her?

Algiers has an influence on women – Bruce dressing as a boy, Catherine playing the actress, me on the terrace with my wine, my delirious imaginings. Each of us has found our refuge – lies, seduction, fantasising.

Bruce's frustration at not being a boy, her eyes fixed on Erwan; I must separate them.

Guilt at having abandoned Bruce to her foolish whim, left her alone in the street; she was in such a hurry to leave, as if she had stolen something. I must call Catherine and check.

In the caves of Tassili, children who have no childhood appear in the paintings among the hunters, warriors, animals, in mountains, crevasses, marshlands. Children caught up in the violence of men, of geography, of irresistible forces, in violent storms.

Scenes of life and death recreated often by women in memory of who they were, who we have been, what we are, what we will become.

Scenes etched by way of warning: rage will not vanish, it lies in wait, resurfaces, it will return.

Scenes that cannot be eradicated, that throw light on the past and darken the fate of humanity.

The hum of the television in the background. I am lulled by the sounds of the Arabic language in the presenter's voice, I experience afresh the reality of living abroad, the feeling of not being from this place, of starting from scratch, having to construct everything – my house, my garden, my son's upbringing, my husband's desire. Our first years together are a blank; all I remember is realising that I'd made a mistake.

I pick up the phone, check the connection; Erwan assures me he's given Bruce our number.

Erwan, the lover transfixed.

Watching Bruce as she spits from the highest branch of the fig tree, demonstrating her power, her superiority over my son. Erwan not daring to say a word or show his admiration in any way in my presence.

My son, my daughter. Erwan, The River.

Longing, despite everything, to hear Catherine's voice. I dream of inviting her here, of cooking for her, casting aside my domestic habits, replacing them with the habit of her skin, her words, her stories, her men — if they exist — and making them mine too, so I can leave behind the brutal world of imagined sailors and dockers and rise to her level. I who am not loved enough.

Writing this, I'm not being fair to Brahim; his love for me is so great that he is willing to accept distance, the loss of desire. He doesn't expect, he carries on. He works for all of us, for the house. He gives me money to do the shopping without humiliating me; he protects me, as a man believes he must protect the woman he loves, the woman who keeps his home.

Undying love, promised in the presence of witnesses.

I betray him slowly, step by step, just as I climb the stairs in the Bousbas' apartment building. I should be content with my lot. I yearn for something, I don't know what, I want something to happen, for good or ill, I want my existence to take on a meaning. If I have to throw myself into the arms of the devil to give my life meaning, I will.

I must phone Catherine to ask about Bruce, for myself.

I make the call.

She was about to phone me (not true). We have a tacit understanding. Our children bring us together despite our different needs. I entertain her, she fascinates me. Tomorrow, Blida, the countryside, together. Brahim declines the invitation to come with us, he'd rather stay home and plan our next trip to Bou Saada. I know he's lying, I don't object.

I'd rather hear lies than the truth.

Fields of giant daisies. Bruce and Erwan vanish among the flowers. The daisies grow thick, their long, ridged stems oozing sap when they snap – the field is alive. The sticky plants slow our progress, we have to fight them off, like children struggling in our arms.

Catherine places her hand on my shoulder to stop herself from falling, forcing me to play the man, protect her; I am at home here, I share nature's violence.

Rain overnight, the smell of wet earth, light bouncing off the rocks, our hands torn by the daisies. To lick Catherine's blood, become as she is. I could never be mother to Bruce.

The children run wild in the field, we'll lose track of them, leave them to their races, their wrestling, their unnatural love.

Erwan and Bruce.

Letting off steam, yelling, fighting, the giant daisies inflaming their desire for each other, Bruce hating Erwan, Erwan hating Bruce, resenting each other for their impossible affair, their forbidden union.

There's no future for them, they'll part, despise each other, lose touch, they won't be reunited, everything that connects them will vanish. All their desires, for murder, triumph, madness, will be extinguished; the cruelty of childhood, Algeria's influence on our lives, it will all fade. I would not be the woman I've become if I'd stayed in France. Erwan would be a different child. But Catherine will leave, taking Bruce to other lands, other triumphs, other tragedies; I shall never know how much she has been changed by Algeria, how much it has altered her nature.

We could be kidnapped by peasants. They'd let the children go, keep us as sex slaves. Catherine would be the most coveted, the most in demand, I'd watch her suffer, take pleasure in her pain.

My insane imaginings.

I feel no shame for my thoughts, they are purified by my journals; as soon as I write them down, they become less tainted, less alien. The words I pluck from my inner being are adornments. Bruce has understood this too; she fills her notepads, delivers her blasphemies, hoping her words will be read, that she will be saved.

Erwan talked to me of his own accord while we were in the car, waiting for Bruce and Catherine in the central square of Blida. He told me about one of their games – how they'd arranged cushions and pillows on the bed and the small sofa in Erwan's room and played 'bordello', each selecting a prostitute for their own pleasure. He doesn't seem surprised that Bruce played the role of a man, a client, projecting his desires onto a woman; the two children, mirror images of one another, cast as young men in the game.

My son – his candour, his urges.

Mud, slush, snails, the field is a battleground, we don't walk through it, we propel ourselves forward, our muscles stretched to the limit by the gigantic flowers, limbs sinking into the sodden grass, the Algerian countryside is a jungle after the storm. This land must be worked for, learnt, revered – virgin soil still, despite all the history, the region razed, pillaged, burnt during the war, villages and resistance strongpoints crushed and now abandoned.

I've brought my secateurs, I cut us a path, the children, delirious, have gone on ahead, their voices circling, weaving together, I can no longer tell which is which. Twin brothers.

The more I cut the giant flowers that block our way, the more Catherine opens up to me.

Amar will be back from his travels soon, he was in Central Africa, she dreads his homecomings, when he comes back from the oil rigs he's 'ready to explode', he's all over her like an animal (her words), it didn't turn her off before, quite the opposite, she had no inhibitions, she was quite turned on by it all (I'm embarrassed by this confession), but she's seeing someone at the moment and she finds it difficult to satisfy them both, to juggle their preferences, her husband's and her lover's – she has to kill off one in her mind to maintain her self-respect.

She's always known how to be with men, from secondary school onward men liked her, enjoyed her, she had fun with them, made use of them, then she made the great leap into marriage, fidelity, she wanted to try it, but she's never managed to be faithful to Amar; she preferred him to other men, she married him because he was unfaithful too, she thought he'd understand. But men, even those who are unfaithful, want to be the only one – the male, the progenitor, the boss – they don't want to share.

When Bruce was born, Amar was suspicious. Catherine swears he's the father, and, anyway, Bruce looks like him – she has his eyes, his mouth, his gestures. She's always wanted to be like her father, from the very beginning, him or another man just like him, with his shoes, his clothes, his hairstyle.

Catherine allowed her daughter to do as she pleased, she was surprised, amused by her, she finds it touching, even though she knows that it will be painful for Bruce.

Suffering is part of women's lot.

Catherine is afraid she might have shocked me. I reassure her, if anything I find it rather sad. I have a vision of myself in my chequered apron, scouring fish heads – sea bream, rock cod – scraping the scales from the gleaming fatty salmon flesh, chopping the heads off tiny sardines before frying them up. I know nothing about men, only my fantasies. Brahim is the first, he will be the last.

Catherine in the field of giant daisies, she looks like an animal. If I were to take a Polaroid of her body, the image would reveal nothing human.

Sexual confidences.

Sensing that she feels sorry for me, pities me.

I imagine her being passed around in the back alleys of Algiers, her skin blackened with grime and sweat, hair matted with spittle, on her knees, on all fours, insatiable and humiliated, hungering and fallen, a feverish look in her eyes, her lips bruised and torn.

Bruce's make-believe brothel or her mother's bedroom?

She's scared too that Amar will be violent with her daughter. It could happen – a slap, the belt – he sees her as a rival, she provokes him, the masculine role model, the positive and negative father figure she doesn't respect and who has robbed her of her mother.

Catherine will leave one day, with no warning, she's sure of it, unless Amar finds another job elsewhere – his oil company has bases all over the world – she'd go with him, she's losing him but she still loves him – absence, that palace of delights.

When Amar returns from his travels and if she doesn't have a lover at the time, she readies herself for her husband like a bride, offers herself to him like a mistress, misses the days spent alone with her child.

Catherine belongs to all men, she's not mine. Then, she says of Brahim: 'You two don't seem very well-suited.'

I don't respond. Holly, nettles, flowers that sting, spiky roses, I hack at anything that will hurt and punish me for not contradicting her.

Branches of dry trees like antennae receiving messages from the dead.

On our way back to Algiers I follow closely behind Catherine's car – I'm like the driver of the Renault 8, following a woman, forcing her to speed up, cause an accident. Erwan falls asleep in the back seat, the air is thick, clammy, there's more rain on the way. I try and find an Italian radio station but all I can hear is static, an inaudible frequency, a disembodied voice trying to warn us.

We reach the outskirts of the city and go our separate ways, Catherine drives faster than I do; I'm afraid of seeing Brahim again since she made that barbed remark: 'You two aren't well-suited'.

Our house seems smaller than usual, pieces of broken glass are scattered on the road, a visitor, the wind, a squirrel. I park outside, wake Erwan from his dreams of aircraft carriers and battles. The skies open, a torrent of mud streams down from the Shell building; I imagine it sweeping along Catherine's dresses, make-up, underwear, Bruce's corrupt soul.

The house is empty, Brahim has gone, on the dining room table he's left a road map, plane tickets, a leaflet from our hotel in Bou Saada. There's a light on in the living room, our bedroom. The garage is empty, his car is gone.

I believe that thoughts can travel, he must have heard Catherine chipping away at the cornerstone of our marriage, shining light on our silence, 'not well-suited' – out of step, pulling in opposite directions, away from the path of desire and the union it brings.

I wait for him.

My man, my husband.

I despise Catherine.

I reassure Erwan, no need to worry, his father will be back, he's probably gone to do an errand.

I drink some wine and the burden of waiting is lifted. Algiers rears up like a construction set, weathervanes spin in the wind, cranes sway, sheets take flight, ships reel towards the horizon and vanish into the void.

Catherine. Her safari jacket, linen trousers tucked into rubber boots, blonde locks; relaxing in haunts unknown to me, drinking fiery spirits, her features distorted by the swirling cigarette smoke.

Alcohol leads to madness.

A Serge Reggiani record plays on the turntable, 'Ma liberté'.

Cut up the tomatoes, chop the basil, grate the cheese, boil the pasta. Erwan watches me, he's exhausted. I've pulled myself together, the mother hen in the kitchen, wifely gestures that save me from terror, give me a part to play. This is how my son will remember me – at the stove, sorting, rinsing, chopping, fish blood on my hands, the smell of chicken in my hair and on my clothes, removing gristle from cuts of meat, bœuf bourguignon, jacket potatoes ('Wearing their coats,' Erwan says), artichokes with vinaigrette sauce, home-made chips, banana bread, chocolate pound cake, crêpes Suzette, kidneys for iron, blood oranges for vitamins, chocolate milk, toast, still trying to master glazes, sauces, aubergines confites, quince jelly – working to perfect my role as mother to make up for my failure in my role as wife.

Raindrops splashing on the roof of our house. Through the bedroom curtains the garden is awash — rocks, grasses, flowering vines where we sip wine in the evening. Erwan sleeps, we could live together, just the two of us, and never go out. I'd watch my son grow like a plant, he'd become a man, take Brahim's place, I'd be at his command, waiting for him in the evening, a symbolic wife who neither kisses nor hugs her one and only son.

During the night, the sound of the car, the garage door, a key in the lock. I don't stir. Brahim gets into bed beside me, turns me over onto my back, lifts my nightshirt, forces his hand between my legs. I say nothing.

VI

Parallel connections. Catherine and me, Bruce and Erwan.

After school I drive Erwan and Bruce to the Shell building, site of my fantasies, its power now weakened by familiarity. Catherine is expecting us.

The gatekeeper greets me, I drive up the ramp and park in my spot, Amar's space under the awning.

I fill Catherine's hours for her; Erwan fills the seconds for Bruce, who is harsh, aggressive, demanding.

The children are waging a war of nerves: they play horses, motorbikes, they shout, maddened by repressed desire and loathing. They echo each other's way of speaking and walking, hitting the walls of Bruce's bedroom with boxing gloves, throwing the nunchucks, breaking a pane of glass. They sniff, spit, scratch, lie beaten on the floor drawing circles in ever increasing numbers, spiralling together, red suns, black moons, tracing lines we cannot see, lines we cannot grasp, cannot understand.

It's an unequal battle – Erwan will grow into a young

man, Bruce will either remain as she is, frozen, or undergo a transformation. She is angry, resentful of Erwan, she hits out at him, he staves off her blows, he learns from her, takes everything from her, twisting and turning beneath the Bruce Lee posters, disgusted at having been seen as a weakling, a girl. He could crush her with his fist, he'll never do it, he wouldn't dare. The future is his; fast though Bruce may run, Erwan will outrun her. He'll fall in love, have sex — he'll take his place, his rightful place, in the tribe of men.

Bruce, the invert, leading the way. She has a book on sex, she has lent it to Erwan. I flick through the pages, imagine them being most drawn to the centre spread, an image in black and white of a naked couple, the man lying on top of the woman. Erwan sees himself as the man, Bruce doesn't identify with the woman.

There is only one woman: her mother.

Catherine's hands as she does her nails, blows on the polish to dry it.

Her long suede skirt, cinched tightly at the waist, the curve of her hips.

V-neck jumpers, fine gold chains around her neck.

The timbre of her voice, elegant and mocking.

Is it only in my presence that she doesn't answer the phone? Or in her daughter's presence too?

She would like to get to know every continent, the men of each one.

Her body, for all men, but still her own.

Men are in thrall to her, but she is in thrall to no one.

Women who devote themselves to seducing men; self-desire, refracted through men.

Amar will come back from his travels with gifts for her, lingerie, a pair of high heels. He knows her size, he is his wife's man.

I want to bathe in Catherine's blood, lose myself in her story, go back to the origin of women, find my own history, who I was, who I could have become. I want to be in her arms, find consolation for not being other than I am.

She advises me to change my hairstyle, the way I dress. She does my make-up, runs her hand over my cheek, sometimes I am the beggar's little dog, sometimes Erwan's mother. When our children are with us, my desire for her is muted, deflected. I look beyond her, to her men, to the unseen, to things that don't exist, things that will never come about.

Is she aware of her own gestures towards me – taking my hand, touching my shoulder, brushing her fingers on my skin – or is this her feminine body language, applied indiscriminately? Men are the only temptation, the target. She has no need of her relationship with me. I'm expendable.

She comes to the house when Brahim is out; looking at her on the steps to the terrace I think I'm seeing a figment of my imaginings until I gradually become accustomed to her presence in my space, the feeling of being inhabited by her.

Standing beside my garden, dismantling it with her presence, as if both had lost their meaning, cancelled each other out. She never sets foot in Erwan's room, nor in my bedroom, she refuses to see the backdrop to Bruce's visits to our house, the room where Brahim is centre stage when we sleep together.

My cakes, my offerings. But like her daughter, she eats like a bird. Women refuse food, choosing instead to give it to their offspring – control and sacrifice.

Memories of wars and famines, women's bodies as reserves of flesh – breasts, hips, thighs, milk – a reminder of all that families, that peoples, have suffered.

She never pays Erwan any compliments. When I sing Bruce's praises, she knows that I'm lying, that her daughter upsets me, that I'm shocked by her. I'm behind the times compared to her, old-fashioned, provincial.

When we go to Bou Saada, she'll be in Paris with Bruce, with her husband. I can picture them there, refusing to go back to Algiers, there's nothing to hold them here. Paris versus the Algerian desert.

The sky brings us together, from her building to my house, a short journey that I shall still be making while she discovers a new city.

Algeria is my destiny. I wasn't to know this as a child.

One evening. I drive her home with Bruce – Erwan isn't with us – past the gates, up the hill, I drop them in front of their block. On the way out I stop after the ramp, get out of the car and walk across a courtyard; it's almost dark, I have an urge to walk around the gardens, the park beckons to me. I take one of the paths, come to a paved area where men lie in the sun on summer days, naked, limbs entangled, on top of each other, bodies, floppy and plump, hard as stone, muscular, twisting, intertwining, away from the gaze of women.

By day, the gardens seem more distant, as if they've receded during the night, moved away from the building. Catherine stays inside, I watch over Erwan and Bruce as they run along the dirt paths and dive into the long grass, waves of green that sway and ripple in the breeze, grazing knees and elbows as they collide, tumble into brambles, nettles, bark, sparring with the landscape itself, challenging the earth, the trees; nothing can resist them, everything must bow to the violent energy that they drain to the last drop, only for it to surge again more furiously than before. Catherine watches us from the top floor, queen of her domain; my body must seem so small to her from up there. We are nothing, our stories come and go, families are born and die, friendships are formed and broken, love is born, flounders.

Amar has come home from his travels. Catherine wants to introduce us. I'm wary of meeting him, afraid of what he'll think of me, of Brahim, afraid of discovering another side to Catherine; her husband might show her in a different light, I might not recognise her, I'd feel let down.

Erwan is invited too.

Everything could seem unfamiliar to me, I'd feel compelled to hide behind my son, my husband, embarrassed, awkward. I've lost the habit of being in a group, my relationships are all one on one – intimate, destructive.

160

Brahim wants to go out, we never invite his friends over any more, the house has closed in around us, because of me, because of the wine, because of the garden and its hypnotic magnetism that keeps us prisoner, forces us to wonder at it, watch over its blooms, its cycle of birth and decay, because of the city, Algiers, loud, aggressive, over-crowded.

I'm afraid I'll be ashamed of Brahim, I hate writing this, but it's the truth. Ashamed of the way he dresses, the things he says, as if nothing about me is good enough, as if Amar were bound to be better than Brahim.

Dress, skirt or trousers? Whatever I do, Catherine will look better, she always does. I'm not jealous, I'd like to have her gift, everything suits her, hangs beautifully on her, cleaves to her as her tongue must to her lover's when their lips meet in a deep, sexual kiss.

Black dress, long sleeves, high neck, like a convent girl, innocent of all desire. Little girls on city streets, invisible, untouched by men's corruption, by their impatience, men who are the masters of the city's walls and roads, to whom the city belongs, murderers of youth and purity. Little girls who forge ahead, rise above the crowd to claim their place at university, their student rooms, who dream of moving on, of leaving the land of madmen.

Sheer tights, invisible, for Brahim's fingers to brush as I sit beside him in the car. But not now, not since the last time; he feels ashamed.

Earrings, hair, a touch of make-up. I'm not skilled at these things, I have no desire to wear make-up, I'm not involved in women's things, in being attractive to men. All I know is my garden, tending it, working it, I've walked away from civilisation, I am stone, I am the plant that grows in stony soil.

Brahim, suit, shirt, burgundy wool tie. His hair is longer, his beard thick, trimmed, salt and pepper, neither young nor old, in his forties. The age when you know how much you don't know, when you accept the mistakes you've made but are still prepared to make more because you know you have to keep trying, keep searching. The age when the body is still firm, well-defined, athletic but without the arrogance of youth; when the lower back is beginning to lose strength (a touching weakness) but the body is still radiant, splendid, inspiring confidence.

My beloved Erwan with his blazer, his shirt, his trousers that are too big for him.

Dressed for a wedding. I take a Polaroid of myself in the mirror, in the picture I look like I'm pointing a gun.

We hardly ever leave Hydra at night; outside, beyond our little world, I feel excited. We don't have far to go, in the darkness the mimosas loom large, bursting out of the garden, swelling to form a natural barrier, impenetrable.

In front of the Shell building with Brahim, a feeling of transgression, needing a drink.

The lift isn't working, we walk up the stairs in single file, as we did at the cove, heading either for a festive evening or a disaster, our disaster. What if all the various elements of our story, suddenly brought together, were to destroy our unity, shatter the (illusory) harmony, uncover the deception — my desire for Catherine, my husband's loneliness, Bruce's hatred for Erwan, the Bousbas' adultery?

Catherine comes to the door. Loose red top, jeans, flip-flops, a coral necklace — we're overdressed.

Brahim's sheepish smile, his suit and tie, my dress, we have to put on an act, we do it often enough. Erwan runs straight for Bruce's room without saying hello, already peeling off his blazer.

I hold out the crocuses from the garden for Catherine, Amar joins her.

Black hair, full lips, he's wearing a shirt with the sleeves rolled up, no watch, no wedding ring, slim-fitting trousers, boots, the same animal grace Bruce has. Not as I imagined him.

Catherine and Amar, the perfect couple, at ease in their bodies, relaxed about our apologies. I'm crying out for a drink.

Bruce comes over to say hello, she's wearing shorts and an old T-shirt, bare feet, she's made no effort, she looks like she's been crying.

The guests in the living room don't turn around to greet us. Four men, four women, friends of the Bousbas', they arrived earlier, lying on the rug, on cushions, talking loudly with the ease of people who feel at home, confident, sure of their image, their opinions, animated by the wine, the whisky, the music.

The apartment is unrecognisable. Catherine has moved the armchairs and coffee table aside, put up a buffet table at the back of the empty dining room – wine, spirits, water, lemonade and bread to one side, a platter to the other, where the slaughtered lamb will be placed, a fresh carcass, not yet putrefying.

I pour myself a glass of wine while Catherine is out of the room, Brahim joins the men on the rug, he's taken off his jacket and tie, he thinks he's among friends, but he's not, he's not like them, because of me, the garden, the evenings alone, the city in tears.

Amar brings up the subject of Erwan and Bruce's friendship, he mentions the sheriff's badge, the day at the beach, how gentle my son is according to Catherine, how rough his daughter is, my house – he'd like to have a look at it, to get an idea, although an apartment is more secure.

Algeria is a subject of discussion abroad, he says, there's an air of uncertainty, something is brewing, with the Libyans, the Syrians and maybe the Iraqis, the Ayatollah has sons all over the world, they'll have sons who'll have yet more sons. Children of violence, he believes. I imagine him seeing the pent-up violence in me, associating it with the country's coming fall.

Earlier, I was contemplating my plants, now my gaze is turned to people, their gestures, voices, laughter – carefree people, flowers of the cities, resplendent with light and colour, fruit of this earth that will soon be caught up in a cataclysm, buried under a rain of blood.

Catherine's hand around my waist, a gesture of affection, explaining our presence. Brahim and I are out of place here.

I've never seen him dance. Salome, dancing in the flames.

Bruce's room is empty, the children have occupied the parents' bedroom, a television plugged in for the evening, they're quiet, watching an episode of *La Piste aux étoiles*, as if the presence of these other adults prevents them from giving vent to their violence. Brother and sister in front of the television; they'll go to sleep in each other's arms.

We're leaving for Bou Saada in two days, we shouldn't have come, we should be home making preparations for our trip to the desert, cleansing ourselves of impure thoughts. I should be purging myself of Catherine's corrupt heart, not communing here with the ghosts of the Shell building, with phantom spirits of massacres and carnage.

Writing in the desert as an act of purification.

Sitting on Bruce's bed, surrounded by posters, waiting for a sign from the Kung Fu master; he stays there, frozen in paper and Sellotape. Bruce sits down beside me. Together we admire her idol, praying for him to rest in paradise and not in hell. Together in silence. Across her left thigh, a large bruise.

Another glass of wine.

The lamb is brought in, carried on the shoulder of the man of the house, Amar triumphant, back with his wife. The creature's legs are swollen from the cooking process, skin rolled back to the bone, head sliced open, blood vessels, nerves, belly slit and stuffed with herbs, garlic, onion, the animal embalmed, served up for the guests to tear into with their fingers, to feed on, savouring the taste of the cadaver that could very well be the corpse of a small boy.

The rumble of voices grows louder, drowning out the sound of the wind in the branches of the forest that surrounds the French Embassy.

The building sways, rights itself, the effect of alcohol combined with the feeling of being out of place at this soirée, of not belonging to the social class of the guests, of being on a different path. Catherine is wrong about Brahim and me: we may have moved apart but we are on the same path, with me just a little ahead, beyond the point where our love became dislocated.

Gilberto Gil.

One of the women, recently returned from the US, compares the liberation of black Americans to the Algerian liberation; she believes in a pan-African state, a dynasty of the oppressed, the children of slaves rising up against the capitalist order; the next revolution will be a women's revolution, violence is a collective experience, men will be free when they have understood and absorbed this: all men and all women, equal.

Catherine doesn't like politics, she prefers music.

Shirley Bassey.

Jiyed, Amar's best friend, is a believer in the virtues of poetry: before they overthrow their government people need to be educated, instructed in beauty.

The country's rich resources – oil, uranium – and power cuts, says Amar.

The secret services have infiltrated intellectual circles, either to spy on them or to make use of them.

It's not enough to provide medicines for the people, they need love, they'll turn to religious leaders, no one else is giving away bread and milk.

A psychiatrist was paid a visit by the militia, they looked through his files, made a note of his patients' names, only God has the right to probe and heal troubled minds.

A man was arrested in Algiers for sticking needles into women's thighs, women wearing skirts.

Laughter and whisky.

Resisting the temptation to go and join the children, embarrass myself, sacrifice Brahim's honour.

My husband is the lamb, being butchered and devoured.

Greasy lips and fingers.

Catherine's neighbours have received threats, a piece of paper folded into four, no envelope, slipped into their letter box, spelling out in detail the abuse to be meted out to them.

Another glass of wine. One last one.

Brahim has put his jacket back on, his tie dangling from the pocket, the men go out on the terrace to smoke. A starless night. The Shell building, a nuclear shelter for a war that is yet to come, a war feared by some, expected and hoped for by others.

The players have scattered, I'm left standing centre stage, I could drill a hole to spy on the neighbours below, the ones who received the threats, the ones who will be the first to leave.

The list of the future dead.

They dance like my son's little Chinese skeleton.

Catherine is lost to me. But had I ever found her?

I'm cold, Erwan is tired, it's time to wind up our evening, relieve the guests of our company, mine especially; Brahim can't make up his mind, he never can.

Liberation will begin here, when we take our leave of Amar and his wife, the sham couple and their friends, the mock revolutionaries.

Rage fuelled by wine.

I go into the bathroom, splash water on my face, the back of my neck. In the hallway, I hear someone ask Catherine who I am. She replies: 'She's a bit unhinged, but very sweet.'

Wine, words and images echoing, lights flashing. Brahim puts his arm around my shoulders – am I that unsteady on my feet? Or is it a loving gesture for his wife, unaware of the deranged state of her mind, her melancholy belief that she is in love – the woman bent on her own destruction?

On the staircase, in single file, hand in hand, three pilgrims; the promised land, if it exists, undiscovered by us.

Bou Saada. Sand dunes, snaking to infinity, with no beginning and no end. This is where we found the seeds of the small palm tree in our garden, we're returning to the place of its birth.

I haven't seen Catherine again, I haven't called her. They're in Paris.

What did Catherine mean by 'unhinged' and 'sweet'? Unhinged like a door that's come off its hinges, sweet like a performing dog.

Sorrow and shame.

Sorrow of betrayal, shame that follows wine.

Our hotel is built on several levels, alternating light and shade. The bottom level, a space of flowers and trees that circulates the air my lungs crave. Brahim's gentleness is weighing me down, I can't respond to it, I can't analyse my feelings. The love I feel for him is a love without substance, or perhaps I love him through Erwan, son of the father. Family connections are tentacles attached to organisms. Loving Erwan forces me to love Brahim.

I write in our room, the desert is an ocean.

Brahim leaves early in the morning with Erwan, their camel rides booked the night before. Brahim walks beside the camel driver, their route marked out. What do they talk about? Sand dunes that look like waves? Drought? Poverty? The city the people from this region flee because of the racist attitudes of the northerners? His wife whom he doesn't understand? His son growing up in a country without a future?

Catherine knows I heard what she said about me. She must be embarrassed, or relieved perhaps. I could make her confess. I've thought about writing an anonymous message, for revenge, a letter like the one her neighbours received: 'We're going to slit your throats, all three of you. You, your daughter and your husband.' I'm despicable.

Living with the possibility of being murdered.

Algeria. I'm going mad. Brahim is a shadow. My son must leave. We, his parents, will stay.

The desert is hostile, I could lose my way here; the desert is generous, healing, its light is the balm, its air the mantle, its palm grove the city of happiness that envelops me, where no one knows me, no one recognises me. The men of the desert don't look at French women.

I picture Catherine in Paris, restored to her rightful place in society, following her desires, pursuing affairs, a life of fragments that together will make up a full existence when she reflects back on them one day.

On the streets of Paris, sure of herself, far away from Algeria, its crowds, the sombre times.

Michèle Akli, the lady-in-waiting.

I imagine Bruce striding confidently along the Champs-Élysées, the capital opening its doors to her, welcoming her kind, children who are neither boy nor girl, troubled waters. Paris, department stores, Christmas decorations, a world away from the country of men who dislike women.

Alone in the hotel room in Bou Saada, I imagine being on a retreat. I could live without Brahim; I could live without Erwan if I knew he was safe somewhere, far away from this country.

Sand spiralling upwards in a column of air, the colour of the sky as the sand rises to meet it.

Faces swathed in scarves, skin stained from dye.

The women of the desert have more freedom than women in the cities.

The beauty of the desert dwellers, their skin so different from mine, their features. Boubous, gandouras, jewellery, Tuareg rings and amulets.

I try and find love for Brahim, pray that I will be overwhelmed by beauty, that it will lead me back to the man I've neglected. I watch him as he sleeps, bathes, gets dressed, leaves the room, his jacket, trousers and jumper, my hand could reach out and caress him, spark life into his skin, make it one with mine. I cannot bring myself back to desire, I have been cast adrift.

My son is my consolation.

Erwan, hope.

Brahim, my protector. I have an interview for the job as librarian at the French lycée. The cultural attaché will talk to me in April when he takes up his post. His name is Henri Thomas.

Men on horseback. Twenty of them together in a group, their saddles decorated with silver thread, dressed in baggy trousers, boots, burnous, gold lamé headdress, all brandishing rifles. The horses rear up, impatient for the chase, their coats brushed, gleaming, muscles taut. A gunshot, the horses surge forward, their riders borne along, weapons in one hand, reins in the other, backs arched, braced against the speed, pulling hard on the reins. The sky is red with burnt gunpowder. Fantasia. It's 1978, the first day of January.

A cross chalked on our gate. We clean it off. No sign of intruders in the garden, no footprints in the soil, no plants trampled, the garage is shut. The front door is open. The stereo is still there, the television too, nothing seems out of place in Erwan's room, my jewellery is still in its boxes, clothes, records, photographs are all where they should be – there's nothing missing. My notebooks have been pulled out of the drawer in my bedside table, they seem to be out of order but I can't be sure, maybe I rearranged them myself before we left. Brahim calls out to me from the kitchen. On the table, a glass of milk and a piece of bread – a prowler, a gentleman.

I'm frightened. Our house has been marked. They'll come back.

The militia.

I check the doors, the locks, the garden, the garage.

When I answer the phone, I listen for a sound that could prove to me that we've been bugged.

I speak softly, inspect the pictures on the walls, the frames, mirrors. In town, I look out for spies, assassins waiting for the right moment to come back and annihilate us.

I miss Catherine. I don't call her.

Outside the school, the Citroën CX. Bruce waves from a distance, she doesn't come any closer, pays no attention to Erwan. I stay in the car, I don't ask Erwan about his friend, about their friendship petering out, I keep my own affairs out of his. I'm in the dark.

It has snowed. Flowers are imprisoned in ice, native species, frozen organisms that will come back to life in a new era.

Since the break-in, I've felt that I'm writing with someone looking over my shoulder, checking the content of my thoughts, judging them.

Chocolate mousse, the Moulinex whisk, fragile egg whites that flop as they start to froth, then foam up and rise again, their texture like a dancer's tutu.

I fall asleep chastely in Brahim's arms, desiring only to be protected by him. Terrible visions of his body, battered and bloody, the unbearable sight of him on his knees, tortured, humiliated.

Catherine phoned. She's given in. Out of boredom, regret. We're invited for a Wednesday afternoon, Erwan and me, to her place, Amar is away again, she has some gifts for us from Paris. I accept the invitation for Erwan, not for myself.

My chequered skirt.

In Baïnem forest, hazelnuts, chestnuts, holly, thistles.

As I drive out of the garage I check to see if we're being followed. Instead of going straight to the Shell building, I take a detour through Place d'Hydra and post a letter to my parents and my brother sending them my love together with a photo of Erwan holding a spray of mimosas, his face obscured by blooms.

My son in the back seat, Alain Souchon on the cassette player: '*Il y a de la rumba dans l'air ce soir.*'

We approach the Shell building. I'm a passenger in a spaceship hurtling towards a star from which it's impossible to return without burning up en route, an astronaut floating in her capsule, lost in the endlessness of infinity, alone, forgotten by all.

We pass the security gate, drive up the ramp. Erwan refuses to take the lift, it scares him. Walking up the stairs, I feel as if I'm retracing my steps from last time. I hear Catherine's words again, confirming our lack of status, the downgrading of our friendship. She treats us less well than the others, particularly me (in my madness).

Outside the apartment. Bruce opens the door.

Catherine gets up from her sofa, embraces me, her hands on my hips, I feel uncomfortable.

In the living room, a winter bouquet, outside, the trees are bare.

She has gifts for us, goes to her bedroom, comes back with a scarf for me, a watch for Erwan, cigars for Brahim, chocolates. Things to make up for the cruelty of the words 'unhinged but sweet'.

She changes her shoes, wants to go for a walk, says it would be good for her. Amar is in Venezuela, contacting him is difficult, he's travelling in the interior, the phone lines aren't good.

Erwan and Bruce make mud bombs and sling them over the barbed-wire fencing that marks the boundary between the gardens and the French Embassy.

The dividing line between French nationals and Algerians. Which side of the fence are our children on?

Daubed on a white wall, an image symbolising the FLN, the Algerian National Liberation Front.

From high up in the building we could be mistaken for four escaped prisoners hiding in the gardens.

Something is going to happen, something will break, be revealed. I have an intuition of an imminent radical change, I feel as if I'm escaping from a trap that hasn't quite snared me.

Away from the shelter of the trees, the wind picks up, almost knocking us over.

On the steps of our terrace, Brahim beside me. Love will return, like a child to their mother, waves to the reef, old age to innocence. Nothing is permanent, not the elements nor the planets that shake us up with their movement, their magnetic vibrations, their warmth. Like them, our feelings revolve, turning back and forth, disappearing, reappearing. From our silent farewells, our kisses will be reborn.

The phone rings. I'm alone, mid-morning, Erwan is at school, Brahim at his factory. Catherine has to go to Mustapha Hosital for a check-up, nothing serious. Bruce needs to be picked up from school right now, she asks me to go and fetch her and keep her here with me while she's out. I can't say no.

Bruce, outside school, her jacket tied around her waist. She runs towards my car, climbs in. We go back to my house.

In the rear-view mirror she looks like a wounded animal found by the roadside, soaked through from the rain, hit by a car or a hunter's stray bullet.

'Yellow Submarine' on the cassette player, Erwan's favourite. No two childhoods are alike. Bruce is lost in thought.

We arrive at my house and she dashes straight to the bathroom and locks herself in. Water running, she's washing herself. She comes back clutching her trousers scrunched up in her hand, asks me to put them in the washing machine and dry them on the radiator. I go and get a pair of trousers from Erwan's wardrobe.

Bruce proudly wearing boys' clothes, hoping her body will take on the characteristics of the body that previously 'occupied' the trousers.

Catherine phones from the hospital to make sure her daughter is with me. It happens sometimes to Bruce, at night usually in her sleep, out of laziness, thinking she can hold it until morning, or when she hangs up after talking to her father on the phone. Catherine has to have a test, she has lost a lot of blood. Bruce is probably scared.

Eyes, hands, hips, shoulders, Bruce's frame.

I daren't take a picture of her, not because I don't want to upset her but because I fear seeing the face of the devil where hers should be in the photo.

I ask her to help me in the garden. I need to dig over some of the soil, cut back an overgrown shrub and prune the medlar tree before spring.

Bruce, the melancholy child.

'Lost a lot of blood.' I imagine them at night, without Amar, sheets bloodied, in the bedroom on the top floor of the Shell building, the ghost ship.

I make us some lunch: crack the eggs, grate the carrots. Bruce is busy in the garden, pulling up the lilacs perhaps, the honeysuckle and wisteria, destroying the dormant rose bushes, the nasturtium seedlings, the fronds of the desert palm tree.

Alone with her. She says nothing, stares at my brooch, my wedding ring, a button on my cardigan, she looks away, unable to hold my gaze, not out of rudeness or shyness, but because she hates the ambivalence of the image reflected back at her.

Errors of nature. I despise myself for writing these words.

Snow is coming, balls of cotton wool hidden in the sky.

For a few hours, Bruce takes Erwan's place; a feeling of being in the presence of a boy and not a girl.

She wants to see her mother, becomes a little girl again, then takes hold of herself.

On the television, an Egyptian soap. Bruce speaks Arabic, understands it, the language of street boys, football players, the language her father speaks in company, as he did at the party, displaying his mastery of the language of power and masculinity, the language for his daughter.

People from Algiers speak French, cling on to the language of schools, universities, colonialism.

Over time, in conversations, one word in French, one word in Arabic, like oil and water, not blending, one liquid stronger than the other.

A few years from now, the dominant language will be Arabic.

The Democratic and Popular Republic of Algeria, as the country we live in is called, the country where we love and stop loving.

She asks for paper and a pen.

I watch her as she writes, bent over, concentrating, using a non-existent alphabet, telling the story of her revenge. She writes of the prison cell that contains her, where she moves about, forging her dreams, where she is sad, happy. She doesn't look human.

Catherine doesn't come into the house when she arrives to collect Bruce, she stays in the car, honks the horn. Bruce goes out to meet her, taking her papers, she thanks me for the trousers, doesn't offer me a kiss.

The sound of their car heading away from the Shell building and towards the city centre that I think of as resembling Catherine's bleeding abdomen.

I feel sad, empty, as if Bruce had inhaled the words from my notebooks and breathed them onto her papers, connecting them with arrows and drawings, giant insects devouring my writing, my thoughts, my soul.

Bruce chose not to go into Erwan's room and select a book, a toy. She stayed with me instead, infusing my blood into hers, ready to transfuse it into her mother's.

I imagine Catherine losing a child, cutting open her veins, cleansing herself of the blood of her lovers.

I wash her glass, her knife and fork, her plate. I wipe down the chair she sat on, throw away the pen that traced lines over mine, letters over my letters, creatures that reflect her disordered mind, like mine. Except that Bruce is not 'sweet'.

Snowflakes fall on the garden, a shower of feathers thrown down by sky-dwellers onto the plants. Sheets from my bed devoid of pleasure, a shroud for the garden. I am the withered tree that will never flower again.

A phone call from Catherine and Bruce, inviting Erwan and me to spend a night in a beach house a few kilometres from Algiers, to say thank you. I'll have to think about it, Catherine presses me to accept.

Brahim says I must go, it will do me good. He wants to be alone, invite a woman over perhaps and replace the ghost of my body with a body that will return his kisses, respond to his lust, take pleasure in his pleasure.

As we are speaking, I think I hear Catherine saying: 'It would be nice to see you again.' Or perhaps she says: 'It would be nice to get together again.'

I drink my wine and imagine Catherine, her belly pressed to mine, her sex against mine, probing inside my mouth, with her tongue, her words.

I call her and say yes, we'll come.

Before, when Brahim used to travel for work, I liked being alone with Erwan. Nights were different, full of wakefulness, freedom. I loved it when Brahim came home too, I'd get dressed up, put on perfume, wait eagerly for him. His absences stood in for love in the game we were playing, made up for what we lacked.

I pack our things, I hate the fact that Erwan and Bruce will be there, I'd rather be alone with Catherine. Clothes for one night, she must have realised – maybe, I don't know.

We follow them by car, driving away from Brahim, from my garden. While I'm gone, seaweed will shoot up, invade our bedroom, suffocate my husband, he won't be alive when we come back.

I don't recognise the coast road, I'm not myself any more, I'm not from here, I despise myself. Bruce's blood flows in my veins, mine in hers. I'm lost.

The sea in winter is not the sea. Its violence forces us to look away. We don't linger at the beach. The breakers could sweep us away. This is no longer Algeria, this is no longer me.

Driftwood, piles of stones, a landscape of fragments.

In the beach house the children have their games, Catherine her beauty, I wait.

I'm ashamed of our overly large suitcase, I don't know how to plan, I know nothing about life. Sadness is an illness. Bruce is wearing Erwan's trousers. I miss Brahim. Catherine opens a bottle of wine. My madness terrifies me.

Hope, that black snake.

Brahim at home, his movements dwarfed by the space when he is there on his own, without me.

Seconds tick by, minutes, I play my part. Impatient for Catherine, waiting to hear her voice.

I cross my hands, hide my wedding ring.

Winter has annihilated the sun.

I wish I knew how Catherine sees me – aside from being the woman with the unhinged mind. I'd like to know if she sees any softness in me or if she thinks of me as being of Bruce's ilk, cruel, faithless.

The children have found some board games in their room, they couldn't open the cupboards, they tried but they're all locked. Who owns this beach house? I don't ask. Two bedrooms, that's all. How will I be able to sleep, so close to Catherine? Intimacy among women is forbidden here. The militia doesn't allow it. I should have said no.

Without Brahim, I feel as if I'm in danger, I feel guilty; my attachment to my husband is based on weakness, lies.

Bruce left her trousers at our house, drying on the radiator; I'll burn them when I get back, to ward off evil spells.

The phantoms of the sea take me far away from myself, so different from the ghosts of my garden that force me back inside myself, like vermin burrowing into the earth.

Out at sea, blocks of ice, broken into a thousand pieces by cargo ships moving through the night, carried on the turbulent waters of the Mediterranean. Catherine doesn't unpack. She looks at me, embarrassed, her beige outfit too elegant for this setting, her hands stilled, barely touching her wine, planning something, I don't know what. How I wish I was included.

Erwan and Bruce, the soundtrack of childhood being stripped from the body, self-destructing, skin being shed, minds cast off.

My notebooks go all the way back to the source of my madness, running the hazardous rapids. I am in an abyss of my own making.

Bruce resists the temptation of love – only her idol has the right to watch her write and sketch, to see her naked in bed, undressed, her femininity restored.

Insane thoughts of Catherine meeting my brother in Paris, of him giving her what I cannot. I could declare myself here, my words drowned out by the noise of the sea. Catherine wouldn't understand, wouldn't be interested.

Two women and two children, nothing could be more fragile, more helpless. If the militia were to show up, we'd be punished for being alone with no men, beaten for being free.

I cast around in my garden for a rare bloom, a flower that is unique, an imaginary species to grow in concert with my words, my thoughts, my gestures as mistress of the house, my expectations that carry no hope. I wait, for nothing, only for my husband to come home from work, my son from school, for the dreams of my youth to return.

Catherine.

She's met someone. A man. He's coming to see her later. She wants to leave Amar, she feels ready, Bruce is a problem, but children have to follow along, bow to passion. I curse the wind, the flooded beach, this beach house devoid of substance. This landscape is a reflection of us. Freedom is an illusion.

Catherine, sitting there in front of me. I prefer the Catherine of my imagination, a landscape of autumn flowers half-hidden beneath the rocks, among the insects, the rotting vegetation. Her face has faded from view, the children's too.

I don't need to respond to her confession. I am not part of her life. Bruce's madness is Catherine's madness, children are born of their mothers, shaped by them alone. The signs of autumn lie under the sand, beneath Catherine's features lies my shameful desire.

The beach house is an animal enclosure, we are the beasts within. Wine coursing through my body, blood pounding in my ears, the apple tart I made, laughter from excited children in the room next door, barricaded in.

The menacing presence of the sea that could rise up like an ocean tide, our ship certain to be wrecked.

Writings of desolation. My notebooks are my memory. Love, like my social standing, has lost its ranking.

Men and women.

Catherine is going out soon, once Bruce falls asleep. She thanks me, tells me I've saved her life (me, the unhinged one). She'll be back before her daughter wakes up. My silence is a frontier that we will not cross.

Alone with the children.

Wine.

Women need men. I see Catherine's world as one of supply and demand.

Erwan has been avenged, I have become Bruce's mother's alibi. Fleeting visions of Amar in a hotel room in Caracas, a city like Algiers, hot and overcrowded. Amar, enjoying the pleasures of the flesh. Catherine, breaking his life apart, love and children following in the woman's wake. She will come back, lost, let down: the dog returns to the leash that restrains it.

In the bedroom, Erwan and Bruce sleeping, like the men in the gardens of the Shell building, sprawled on the ground, sweating, taking what they need from one another, sucking out their lifeblood, sugar, sap, happiness.

Outside, all around the beach house, the night lies dead.

VII

Henri Thomas, the French cultural attaché. We have a meeting, a formality according to Brahim.

He's just taken up his post, he's staying in the Hotel Zeralda, he'll be moving into a new house near the Thomson's gazelle enclosure, the house is still not finished.

He's come here by himself, his wife and two daughters will be joining him soon, at the end of the school year.

He's meeting me at the French Cultural Centre, he'll drive me to the school and introduce me to the staff, show me around the secondary-school library that I'll be in charge of.

My salary will be paid in French francs, the dream currency here.

I don't feel scared, being surrounded by books and secondary-school pupils isn't really a job. The students are protected by writers' words, they are still children. Erwan will start secondary school at the same time, I won't be leaving him.

I'll have time and silence. I'll take my notebooks, I'll write, although I don't want to risk being seen bent over, scribbling. I'm not like Bruce, I'm ashamed of what I write, my ramblings, my body, my face, features deformed by the effort of writing, the meaning of my words.

Spring has washed away the winter, my sadness. I often bump into Catherine after school. We're polite and friendly. I don't go back to her place. When I go to pick up Erwan from the Shell building I wait at the gatehouse, in the shadow of the building. Occasionally, Catherine and I phone each other about the children.

My flowers are blooming early, they look like multi-coloured marbles. My favourites are white, the colour of virginity.

Brahim has painted the shutters red and white, reminis-cent of a holiday villa. The Bou Saada palm tree has given us some dates, Deglet Nour.

Nature has re-established the order I had lost. I feel bored, but the sadness has gone. And most of all, so has Catherine.

When I see her outside school, she's no longer the same woman.

The medlar tree has a few green fruits, they'll start to swell before long, their orange-tinged flesh will be soft and juicy. The bougainvillea has filled out, the façade is com-pletely covered, I'm naïve enough to believe it protects us from intruders, thieves, murderers. But flowers are mute witnesses, not weapons against terror; if they had voices, they would speak in detail of sobbing and violence.

I've decided to wear my yellow crêpe dress for my meeting, with high-heeled sandals.

I've painted my nails, they feel soft when I run them over my lips, unlike my palms which are rough from gardening, cooking, the household tasks – you could read my life in them. These are not the hands for caressing another woman's skin.

The sun is already strong, summer follows hard on spring in Algeria, overlapping with it, spoiling the spring.

I make sure I water the shoots before the sun burns them, they'll be attracting insects again, moths.

A garden is a village, its inhabitants – beetles, salamanders, ladybirds, dragonflies, shrews – are familiar to me, they all return, from their underground home, their country, their hibernation.

Brahim is here, by my side, where he's been all along. I'm back to where I began, my dreams, my gloominess, the silence of the terrace in the evening, our conversations that don't intersect but at least have the virtue of existing.

I'm not happy, I'm not alone.

Catherine seems like a fleeting memory. And yet she does still exist, on the phone, in the Shell building, outside school, in Algiers.

She hasn't left, she's not leaving. Sometimes you think you can die for someone, but that person dies first and leaves a space in your heart, the flames of desire, of rage, no longer fanned. The idea of her has flowed into the river of my thoughts, she is all around me, liquid, without substance. Catherine is neither the root nor the bark of the tree.

Erwan is changing, no longer a faun but still a lamb. Bruce watches him grow, their violence is theirs alone, a secret, I refuse to be witness to it.

The Cultural Centre is in town. I take the car, drive slowly in these sandals. My dress will be crumpled, I'll have to walk around to smooth out the creases. I left early. Late morning, masculine Algiers stirs, the men emerge, stretch, the dockers have been at work for hours already.

Brahim asked me to call him after the meeting, he'll have to wait. I've decided to be more assertive if only because I think it might rekindle my desire; if we feel we're drifting apart, we will be more likely to come together physically at night. I'm conducting an experiment, although I don't really believe in it.

It is impossible to regain what one has never possessed, or only half possessed (Brahim, enabling my fantasies).

I took a picture of the sky before I went out, to bring me luck, there's no reason for Henri Thomas to change his mind, but you never know. The Polaroid captured the cloudless, blue expanse, with the impression of the beating of a bird's wings, quivering, a shadow, diffuse but present.

I see the faces of my brutal, imaginary lovers in the street; if they only knew.

The Cultural Centre occupies three floors of a small building just before La Grande Poste d'Alger. Henri Thomas' office is on the top floor. I check in at reception. An Algerian woman makes a phone call, says I've arrived, asks me to wait, 'He's coming,' she says.

'He', the man, 'coming': to the rescue or to orgasm.

I'm uncomfortable sitting in the imitation-leather chair, my dress will get creased again. I watch the employees going about their tasks, I'm an outsider here, I belong in my garden.

A map of the Sahara is tacked to one of the walls, a map of France too. I stare at them, trying to size them up – the desert, a country bigger than France. I think about the nuclear tests the French carried out during the colonial period in the area around In Salah, mushroom clouds ballooning up from the sand, toxic fallout raining on palm groves, villages, settlements for years to come.

Here he comes (no rescue, no orgasm).

Henri Thomas.

Skirt, bag, sunglasses, heels, Michèle Akli's outfit. Who is this woman? I don't recognise her.

A job to stave off boredom, a boredom that's sometimes enjoyable; time slips by unnoticed when you're lost in admiration for the passing hours, seasons come and go, each one rejuvenating the one before. Nature goes on for ever, while we humans destroy ourselves. None of us will survive, others will take our place.

Henri Thomas is tall and blond (cliché), dressed in a striped shirt, sleeves rolled up, fair hair on his arms, white slacks, broad shoulders, stomach rather prominent, square face, he's strong, I can sense it, a strength that's different from Brahim's, he's a free man.

His hand gripping mine, we exchange greetings, my contract isn't ready yet; we walk out towards my car, no, I don't mind driving us towards the lycée.

Too tall, sitting next to me, thighs, legs, wrists, his voice, too deep.

He fell in love with Algeria three years ago, wanted to work here, couldn't wait to start working here. His wife is French, they have two little girls. He's my age or a bit older, I'm not good at telling a man's age, I don't know men well enough.

He laughs at the end of every sentence, the effusive delight of a happy man, unexpected, surprising, and me, gripping the wheel tightly.

Catherine is the only one who has occupied the passenger seat, I use my car for my family, for my son, occasionally for Bruce, for crates of fruit and vegetables, cartons of milk, bottles of wine, Saïda mineral water.

Congestion in the centre of Algiers, I take the back streets to the French lycée, Henri Thomas holds forth on Algeria as he sees it, the inhabitants, their pride, the beauty of the capital city, the wide open spaces not seen anywhere else, and he's done some travelling, in Asia mostly, nowhere has he encountered a more stubborn people. Nature here carries the imprint of men and women's history, a fortress with weapons to defend itself, the country's lifeblood, more than mere earth and rocks, nature here is flesh and blood.

If soldiers of the militia were to stop us, they would check our identification papers, accuse us of adultery, we would be punished.

The French couple.

If Catherine were to drive by, she would think I'm cheating on Brahim while he's at work at his factory.

If my husband were to see me, he would pat himself on the back, happy to see me changing, coming out of myself, forgetting my woes.

If Erwan saw me, he would think he wouldn't mind having a different father; only mothers are for life.

If Bruce saw me, she would picture herself as Henri Thomas.

The Lycée Descartes, formerly Fromentin, is where General de Gaulle was based. The library where I'm going to work was his office. Walking in the footsteps of history, lost in my fantasy world. I feel small against the immensity of time, the war, peace, the impossibility of reconciliation between peoples.

I park near the main entrance. Henri Thomas greets the security guard, he knows him. Flashback to Catherine and the security guard at the Shell building, a feeling of things being repeated, of being a prisoner of other people's actions, included in an adventure that's not mine, a passive observer, unable to escape.

The pupils are in class. We walk through the grounds, an enchanted fairy-tale forest, unchecked growth spilling over onto the paths and the walls of the classroom buildings, lush, vigorous swathes of banana palms, cactus, baobabs, magnolias, cherry trees, the grounds divided into different zones, a modern structure built during the 1950s for the older pupils, an area with an old chapel and a small Moorish palace for the younger ones.

Erwan will grow up in this idyllic setting, where minds are awakened and knowledge is fuelled by the beauty of the surroundings. He'll make friends, learn, grow into the young man I'm certain he will become. In my mind's eye, I can't see Bruce at his side, she's been removed from the picture, erased.

We visit the Moorish palace with Madame Kuster, the head teacher; a courtyard, a two-storey building rising above it, ten classrooms on each floor. She shows us the library, an old ballroom, a rotunda with an immense chandelier, wood panelling, decorated ceilings, mosaic flooring, the cupola overgrown with roses that seem not to be of this world. Students at work. Walls lined with books, windows of the mind.

We go back to the head's office, Henri Thomas excuses himself, asks if there is a phone he can use. He needs to call the builders working on his house.

I fill in a form – address, phone number, social security number, nationality, bank account for my salary to be paid into. I'll need to open a new account in francs in my own name, separate from my husband's.

Money, a feeling that I'm betraying Brahim. I'll share, we'll use my salary for the occasional trip, presents for Erwan, for clothes you can't find here in Algeria, money to be spent on ourselves, on pleasure, for we know nothing of pleasure, we know only restraint and fear, habits that grind us down and delude us into believing that we will be protected from harm.

Madame Kuster, thick glasses, nylon blouse, skirt below the knee; she'll contact me as soon as my contract is ready, the Cultural Centre manages the school's business affairs. On her desk, attendance registers, application forms, a plan of the new term's timetable. I tell her proudly that my son Erwan will be in the first year of secondary school this year.

Madame Kuster asks if I have any particular requests. Some classes are more 'Arabised' than others – French parents sometimes prefer their children not to mix with native Algerians.

I say thank you but I don't share those concerns. I do ask her for one favour, however: not to place my son Erwan Akli in the same class as Amina Bousba.

The smell of jasmine in the city.

Henri Thomas asks me to give him a lift, he knows we live in Hydra. I can drop him at his still unfinished house, it's not far from where we live. I drive fast, the car speeds up the hill as if jet-propelled.

I've separated Bruce from my son. I see a flash of dust and blood, atoms spinning in space, fragments of stars in the milky way.

Henri Thomas will be in touch soon, when my contract is ready. We'll meet at the Hotel Zeralda, a chance for him to meet my son and my husband, whose voice he already knows from the phone. The swimming pool is heated, it'll be a nice day out.

A happy man. Men like him aren't meant for me.

In the enclosure, a second Thomson's gazelle. I get out of the car and walk towards the fence. The gazelles back away at first and then approach me and lick my hand. Docile creatures trusting me just as my son does. He'd follow me to the ends of the earth, across the oceans, into the bowels of Tipasa, beyond the border into Niger where the desert claims the lives of those who lose their way. My one victory will be that I have kept my true nature hidden from him. A woman will always be mother to her son, the queen who protects, nourishes, witnesses his faltering steps, his falls, his race towards a happiness that won't revolve around her, a happiness she'll embrace from afar, proud of her work; love is the lesson, kisses the education, trust is the key that unlocks the future.

I have given Erwan everything I did not or could not receive. I won't live my life through him but I will always watch him, as I watch the sky in the evening, the Algerian sky and its dying stars.

The new gazelle is smaller, more nervous, a sickly animal; she walks around the enclosure, jostles her partner who rejects her. She has a look that reminds me of Bruce.

On the steps of the terrace with a glass of wine, I imagine Henri Thomas' face burnt by the first of the summer light, like the Asian orchid that won't grow in my garden.

Brahim is happy for me. I tell him about the woods around the school, a haven of tranquillity in the middle of Algiers, the silence of the books, I let him know how grateful I am. I fail to tell him that I love him, we don't embrace.

I unburden myself of my shame and tell him I've separated Bruce and Erwan at school for the new term because I don't want my son becoming a homosexual.

Madness of these words, I'm held in chains by my jealousy.

I hear the sounds of the Shell building again, my head aches, I imagine Bruce in her room pulling down her Bruce Lee posters, ripping up the pages of her notebook, starting a new life of solitude. She doesn't know yet, trusts her intuition.

Henri Thomas' presence in my car, my hatred of men who don't desire me.

Algiers has become a woman, her body smothering mine; my garden is ruined, I no longer exist.

With the intense heat, the fire has rekindled high on the mountain tops, destroying the soft spring wood; the red lines of the fire move in waves, the hills have become erupting volcanoes.

Sometimes in the middle of the afternoon, my clothes soaked with water from the garden hose, I call Catherine. The phone rings in the apartment in the devil's gardens; Bruce's mother doesn't answer, I'd hang up if she did.

Dancing in front of the mirror, trying to see myself as Salome in the flames, I imagine Catherine lost in a village, caught in a trap set by a spurned lover. Her beauty crumbles in the flames, the ashes rise with the clouds of smoke I photograph from my garden.

I learn from Erwan that Amar is in Algiers. The dog has come back to its master, I don't know who's in command and who is meekly obeying.

Our hands are stained red from cherries, mouths stuffed with peaches and apricots swollen with sugar. It's high season, the beginning of summer, the sea still cool.

The end of term is approaching.

Henri Thomas has phoned to say my contract is ready. I've lost the urge to go out to work, but I'll go. I'll be a dog at the beck and call of men: Brahim and the Frenchman on the phone, conspiring together.

The hotel in Zeralda overlooks the beach where I spend my summers with Erwan, the sand dotted with water-logged jellyfish coated in oil from the cargo ships.

The Frenchman has suggested we bring our swimsuits; I won't swim, I'll watch, take pictures with my Polaroid, my madness returned, they'll be embarrassed, Brahim especially.

His unstable wife. Men prefer the company of other men.

In Brahim's car, my son in the back seat, dressed in cut-offs, a white polo shirt, Bruce's sheriff's badge. He's still a child, lost in thought, sulking, his hair uncombed, skin so smooth, already tanned, biceps emerging from tender sinews, manly muscles for which I'm sure Bruce is no match when she tries, still, to hurt him.

I don't feel guilty any more: Catherine's daughter will seek out another Erwan, vampires can always find fresh blood.

The River, my love.

Henri Thomas is waiting for us outside the hotel, smoking with the staff, as if he were the owner, the happy man, at home wherever he is in Algeria.

He calls people 'son', 'my lad', 'my man', talks to the receptionist, the waiter, Brahim, Erwan. He holds the door open for me, sets out our loungers, orders water, Fanta and anisette. He doesn't address me as 'woman'.

'Woman', wife, slave.

We've eaten lunch at home, pizza with tomatoes, anchovies and black olives. Afternoon, the sun beating down, I keep my dress on, I don't want to take my clothes off in front of Henri, it feels too intimate, more so than actually being naked.

The men, my son, in swimming costumes, by the pool. Brahim's muscular buttocks, his sex – I don't know, I can't remember. A wretched thought.

Henri is taller than my husband, Brahim seems to shrink as they talk, a hang-up of the Algerian male in the presence of a Frenchman, my husband's sublime beauty, eclipsed. The Frenchman, relaxed, a little tipsy, the happy man lording it over the man who can't swim.

No one in the pool, no tourists in the hotel, nor anywhere else in Algeria.

Lush growth of bougainvillea, spreading their arms all around us, concealing us from the public beach.

The enclave.

I go inside the hotel, find somewhere to change, a tiny cubicle, I turn the lock, my dress falls down around my ankles, my skin disgusts me, I feel as if it's come loose, it's been so long since it's felt the touch of a caress. How will Henri Thomas see me? He'll probably be indifferent.

Wearing my one-piece, I shield myself behind Erwan as Henri Thomas walks towards me to give me the contract – before he forgets.

Underwater, I disappear.

The men, smoking, debating, drinking.

Erwan jumps off the diving board, dive-bombs, starts again, he wants to go down to the beach, I say no. He's angry about something.

He's bored.

A hotel with no visitors, only us, play-acting at love, friendship. Henri takes Brahim by the shoulders, they talk about the future of the country, religious fanatics, the government, Henri isn't worried, Algeria is a big country, its people independent-minded.

Orange Fanta bubbles explode in my mouth.

Henri's tanned skin.

The world traveller.

The husband with neither wife nor child at his side.

Skimpy swimming trunks, fuzz of hair, stomach muscles faintly outlined – a well-proportioned body despite some heaviness around the waist.

Shoulders filled out in youth.

A man who loves life, embraces life's pleasures.

Temporarily single.

Henri Thomas, lover of a country's beauties, its women, oblivious to my beauty. Madame Akli, untouchable.

Yellow sky, there's a storm brewing, it will break in the night. Fading afternoon light. The water in the pool looks dark through my sunglasses; alligators, snakes, piranhas lie in wait for us in the depths.

The violence of my thoughts, a reflection of my troubled condition.

Erwan: 'I told Bruce yesterday we were going to be here, she'll come, with her mum, we'll play in the pool.'

Another betrayal, like the day at the cove. Is my son getting back at me? Has he sensed that I've separated him from Bruce at school? I smile, tell him it was a good idea to invite his friend.

Henri and Catherine. I remove Brahim from the picture, he doesn't have a role to play in this scene.

She arrives wearing her costume. The bikini she wore at the beach, a red wrap knotted at the waist, coral necklace hanging down to her breasts, stones to protect her beauty. She walks barefoot on the hard ground, coils towards me, spider-like, kisses me on one cheek. 'You again,' she's probably thinking.

Bruce makes straight for the pool, still with her T-shirt on, she must have started to develop, her chest filling out, enough to be noticeable or for her to feel embarrassed. Erwan joins her; friends, inseparable.

Catherine is introduced to Henri Thomas. He smiles. Men are so straightforward. She moves on quickly, joins Brahim. He goes to get her a drink and a lounger; the man, a dog.

Amar couldn't come, he had work to finish, he really wants to see us again, a picnic at the beach perhaps, he'd like that. She's missed me. I don't believe her.

Her beauty. I've missed it.

She radiates life, I speak of the end of days.

Her madness is on display, I hide mine away.

Brahim moves closer to me, distancing himself from Catherine, he's not attracted to her and, besides, he's devoted to his wife, his son, his home. Henri dives, Catherine pays him no attention. She's staring at the two of us, giving us a strange look, of disdain, or curiosity perhaps. Catherine, who can't find a way to stay with Amar, wondering if she'll see in us the answer to her question: is it possible to spend your whole life with the same person?

They arrived late, on purpose, they won't stay long, she just wanted to make an appearance, for Henri Thomas to know of her existence, then she'll vanish and he'll follow her into town, track her to the outskirts of Hydra, to the building with arrow-slit windows.

My paranoia is my poetry, the flowers watch over us.

Catherine doesn't swim. Sitting on the diving board, her legs stretched out over the water, hair loose down her back, she holds her face up to the sky to be judged. I take a picture of her, silhouetted against the light, encircled by a blue halo.

I'm authorised to park in the school car park. I've come to drop off my contract with Madame Kuster. Eucalyptus and mimosa are my escorts. The trees have changed, they've become dry and woody, the sports fields below are deserted, silent, the school is empty except for the older students taking their exams, the others have all left for the summer.

Alone on my way up to the head's office, I'm a little girl in the 1950s again, believing in adventure and desert voyages.

The very air here is French, brought unwittingly by the expat teachers who'll stay for a while and then move on to a new continent, restless, unable to go back home, to France.

The interview is short, Madame Kuster is rushed, she glances through my contract, signs it, puts it in a file marked with my name.

Before I go, she informs me that she has done as I asked regarding my son and Amina Bousba. I leave on a sour note, hoping I never have to see her again.

Evenings of guilt and remorse.

My notebooks of shame.

No wine can bury deep enough, no words can make amends.

Catherine phones me every day, waits for me outside school, invites me to the Shell building where the gardens are cooler than my garden. I don't know what she wants of me.

Expat women, their boredom.

The sofa, coffee, a pear liqueur occasionally, I don't want to drink with her, she'd break down my defences, lead me back to desiring her.

We walk in the gardens with the children, our silence more powerful than words, we have nothing else to say. My secret is safe, the story of Bruce and Erwan is coming to an end, I should be honest and admit that the story of their mothers is ending with it.

The smell of her perfume, the same as on that first day at the beach, when she was Catherine Bousba, a refuge from my sadness, my depression. No one will save me now, not even my son. I have fled towards something that is stronger than I am, something that emanates from within me. I am my own Alien.

If she were seized by an urge to kiss me, I would refuse. I still take pleasure in imagining but she has no such desires and I have no dreams for us. I accept her invitations, next term there will be none.

No one else knows yet. Erwan's attachment to Bruce is stronger than I thought. He'll be disappointed. She was his tree, I'm stopping him from blossoming on her branches. My son is strong, a firmly anchored ship, more flexible than a reed, tougher than a magnolia. He is an extension of my skin; through him, I'll be able to experience all the things I've been denied.

Sometimes we're joined by Amar; he's stopped travelling, he tells us about his travels instead. Catherine must have set out her conditions. He tells us about Easter Island and its mysterious statues, about Benin masks and female healers in the Philippines, about Aztec copper sculptures and the ghost roads of Chile. He is tied to his family, his dossiers, his boredom, he no longer has the oceans, horizons. Catherine will leave him.

Maybe Catherine wants to see me because of Henri Thomas. She mentions him sometimes, asks about the library, my new job, she congratulates me, makes too much of it, she must know I know. She doesn't ask about him, she merely refers to him by his first name once or twice and then says no more.

They're seeing each other behind my back. I have no proof at all. I write it down to give it the weight of truth.

When she's not there, her face is no longer even a memory; eclipsed by the evening in Algiers on the steps of my terrace, like my own face it has ceased to exist.

I accept Catherine's invitation for a day at Moretti Beach, for Erwan's sake. He doesn't know these are his last days with Bruce.

The cooler, hard-boiled eggs and chicken again, fruit and chilled wine.

Days of perfect weather, of artificial pleasures revived, adulterated like my fantasies of brutal lovers.

The beach is dirty, the seawater punishing, the reefs cut like knives. Nature's beauty is an illusion.

We have so many ways of rearranging and camouflaging the brutality of the natural world.

The beach is a remedy for boredom. Desire has gone, in its place there is nothing.

Brahim, driving my car, one arm resting on the rolled-down window, his hand outside buffeted by the wind, the speed. I'm in the passenger seat, my body superimposed on Catherine's, on Henri Thomas'. He won't be there today, he wasn't invited.

Moretti, twelve kilometres from the city, favoured by the Algiers bourgeoisie and gangs of boys who go there to dive off the rocks.

On the cassette player, 'Rockollection'. We sing along to the story of happy young people. I think about the little boys playing football in the street, the sons of Algeria who have seen their fathers weep until they have no more tears to shed. The revolt will be fuelled by the sorrows of the heart. Life cannot be lived without love, without hope.

Moretti. The wind has picked up. Catherine has found a sheltered spot against the wall that divides the beach from the road. Our parasols form a tent, Amar has found some rocks to stabilise them.

Bruce dancing in the swirling wind – Salome, destined to be sacrificed. Erwan joins in. His new-found grace is no match for Bruce's, he dances without skill, unable to find his footing in the bright sunlight. My son is more fragile than Bruce. I have eliminated her to save him.

Atlantis.

I stare out to sea, where the bones of the people we once were lie. Roman ruins are our houses. Our bodies on the beach are the twins of those buried under the sea. Over the centuries we relive the story of our defeats, our mistakes, without repenting for our sins.

Wine.

The children in the water stay close to the shore.

Brahim and Amar, Algerian men.

My husband stands tall, the Frenchman is not here.

Catherine sitting in the shade, curled up, unrecognisable. Who is she thinking about?

She smiles at me.

Fearing for the children, I walk down to the shore. The waves aren't as powerful as I thought. Erwan and Bruce, Thomson's gazelles.

Amar can't do any more travelling. The militia have been investigating him. He's suspected of spying.

Our voices are drowned out by the wind, I hear Catherine talking, but I can't make out what she is saying. I invent words – of affection, regrets, a declaration. My heart is my own, Bruce will take flight, she's like me, she won't be caged.

Amar runs into the sea, dives into the foam, surfaces further out – he's a good swimmer. Catherine pays no attention – her man is a real man. No need for her to look on admiringly.

Wine.

Our children are feeling cold, they roll about on the sand, give each other piggy-backs, like the summer riding on the back of spring.

My garden is overrun by rampant roots, invading the plants, climbing up tree-trunks searching for sunlight. I believe our world is ending.

Amar wants to leave Algeria, he's not afraid for himself, but for Bruce and Catherine. He's put his name down for a transfer. He's expecting to get an appointment abroad.

Without Catherine in the Shell building my garden will no longer exist.

Bruce and Erwan wrestle in the sand, lying one on top of the other, play-acting, recreating the black-and-white photograph in the book, the man on top of the woman.

Amar believed in a new Algeria, it will take time to build a future, to bring the people together and unite them with those who govern, the right man will be needed, a miracle man, an ally of the West, France has abandoned its martyred children, a land that is forgotten and denied is lost.

The Bousba family live near the French Embassy, they thought they'd be able to escape if they had to through the barbed wire. But nothing will save them. Mixed marriages are marriages of traitors.

Bruce alone in the water, on her Lilo, paddling out to sea. The future is hers. She'll be a winner in her game.

Wine.

Catherine is cold, she hasn't taken off her dress, her shoes. We should leave, go back home. Our house is waiting for us. I want to fall asleep in Brahim's arms, dream that we are making love.

Bruce comes running out of the water; a man is drowning.

We hear shouts: 'Help! Help!'

On the shoreline, a group of boys calling, shouting, begging the swimmer to come back. They don't dive in, they're afraid of the waves.

The sea, an inferno.

The cliffs stand inert, nature can do nothing for humans.

Amar runs into the water, dives, another man follows him, Brahim doesn't get up, he can't swim. He lights a cigarette.

I can't see Amar. The sea is rough. The waves have taken control.

Catherine, Bruce, Erwan and me, lined up. A woman, a daughter, friends. A sudden burst of love, fleeting, born of danger.

In the distance, three men struggle against the sea. Amar, the stranger who followed him, the drowning man. Who will return?

For the first time, I put my arms around Catherine, Bruce. The wind, the sand, our bruised skin. Erwan hugs me too. 'What reason could there be for us to need consolation, Erwan?' I say to myself.

They're back. The group of boys pull the drowned man's body out of the water, carry him on their shoulders, place him on the sand. Amar and the stranger join them.

We form a circle, like the pillars of the Tomb of the Christian Woman in Chenoua. The drowned man is young. The boys recite prayers. Bruce stands just outside the circle, holding her father's hand. A trickle of froth runs from the dead man's mouth.

The boys carry him at a run towards the road.

Amar says: 'We tried, it was too late.'

We go back to our spot, under the parasols, stunned. Catherine rubs Amar's skin with a towel.

Brahim says: 'One less Arab.'

A shamed silence.

I don't understand.

Erwan looks at me, I lower my gaze.

I don't understand.

The Bousbas get dressed, gather up their things, go back to their car.

They're leaving. Leaving us.

The garden is in a state of neglect, flowers burnt, withered, rotting, I've let the sun take over. I'm no longer in command.

I write very little. There is no truth at the moment. What could I write about, give permanence to?

Catherine hasn't phoned since the day at Moretti. Bruce has stopped coming over. She's still friends with Erwan at school but I don't think it's the same as before. Unless I'm imagining things. Children don't remember things like we do. The past is soon over and done with.

Wine in the evening, Brahim by my side.

I don't understand.

We can't seem to talk about Moretti. 'One less Arab.' Self-hatred spreading like slime.

The boys at the beach huddled together, their slender legs, long arms, flat stomachs, birds gazing at another bird.

I hate Brahim.

I hate myself for still having moments of loving him, out of pity.

Cracks in the steps on the terrace, I wish I could bury my sorrows in them, the last vestiges of respect, I despise Brahim.

I can't stay here any longer, I can't leave.

Every boy in Algiers has the face of the drowned young man.

The body wrapped in the Muslim shroud.

The mother of this son.

I don't understand Brahim.

Every night, my husband turns over on his side, bends up his legs, clutches his knees in his hands and sobs against his mother's belly.

The school fête. I promised Erwan I'd go, I'm doing it to please him.

It's high summer and I'm cold. Erwan is dressed in a white shirt and beige trousers, he looks like his father in those clothes, the way he carries himself; he won't be the same though, he'll be his own man.

My print dress, red shoes, I've made an effort, I don't want my son to be ashamed of me.

Children, parents, clustering at the foot of the main steps to Erwan's school, hurrying; we linger in the car for a while, Erwan is shy like me, I understand.

We wait.

Lipstick, perfume, I tidy up my hair. Erwan is ready too. We walk up the steps to his school for the last time.

Buffet tables, like the evening of the méchoui at Catherine's. Cakes, sweets, sugar for the children.

Fairy lights strung around the courtyard and along the ramp that leads to the classrooms for the older children, the top class, Erwan's.

Teachers, the head, we say hello.

Inside, the cafeteria has been transformed into a dance hall, reminding me of weddings, communions in Brittany, women dancing together for lack of male partners.

Another buffet, bourek, *choukchouka* salad, sugar-coated tcharak pastries, wine, a jug of sangria.

Children running about, shouting, having fun. The school is transformed.

The night sky is striped with dark patches.

Clouds pass over the moon, making it seems brighter, polished, buffed, all cracks and craters smoothed over.

Rays of moonlight.

Erwan is with a group of children. I don't know anyone here, except a few teachers, the head.

Bruce.

She rushes over to Erwan. They hug then push each other away, brothers.

Bruce is dressed in a blue short-sleeved lace-up blouse, low-cut. Her hair is dripping wet. She comes over to me, I place my hand on her forehead, she's burning up, her skin looks flushed.

Bruce and her madness; other children's madness at this moment.

A stereo system with speakers, loud music. I ask Bruce if she came with Catherine but her answer is drowned out by the noise.

Erwan jumping up and down on the dance floor, he can't dance.

The smell of children, of school, paper, rubber, pencils. My son is no longer a little boy. I'm in his territory, passing through, as if through his childhood. Nothing is left except for a few drawings, snapshots; time steamrollers on, wrenching

215

Erwan from me. My son has gone ahead to the future, I can't join him there, the future has long been out of reach for me.

I look around for Catherine, we haven't seen each other since the day at Moretti.

Someone hands me a glass of sangria: fruit and alcohol, an explosive mixture. I don't want to drink, not in front of Erwan, not here.

I'd rather have wine.

Children, parents crowded together on the dance floor, Bruce and Erwan cling to one another, pushing and pulling, falling over, getting up again, puppy dogs – and I've separated them. I'm not sorry, not any more. Catherine's silence on the subject of Brahim is hurtful.

'One less Arab.' Brahim, shamed on the beach, full of self-loathing, unable to swim, feeling useless, ridiculous. Amar, raised to the status of hero.

My husband never had any desire to learn to swim. I remember being in the sea with him, holding him, buoyed by the water, light, feminised suddenly, ashamed.

A man's sense of honour.

A second glass of sangria. The taste of bad fruit, bad sugar, bad alcohol. I try and find Catherine.

Bruce and Erwan hanging from the bar in the courtyard. Bruce running off, leaving my son alone, holding tight to the bar, not daring to launch himself into space. I leave him alone. Their final games, their last tussles; after the summer holidays they'll be separated.

A third glass of sangria, I'm looking for Catherine.

Men and women dressed up for the school fête, the boredom of Algiers, the lack of entertainment.

Henri Thomas. Walking towards me, he asks if Brahim is with me; no, I say, he was tired. A lie.

Blond fuzz beneath his white shirt; he's wearing a beige jacket, jeans, leather shoes; sexual, not elegant. He's come on his own, he knows the head, he has enrolled his daughters at the school for next term. He likes the tree in the middle of the playground, a poetic touch amid all that cement. I walk away from him.

In my head I hear the sounds of the Shell building, the pillars moving like the legs of a giant alien, striding down from Hydra towards us.

Bruce splashes water on other children from the outdoor basins, almost slips, drinks from the tap, a woman is arguing with her. Catherine.

Wearing a see-through black dress, flat shoes. Her hair like a garment. She's frosty towards me. The day at Moretti no doubt. I go to kiss her cheek, move closer. She steps back, avoiding me.

The dance floor. Erwan on Bruce's back, they're playing horses.

Henri Thomas and Catherine Bousba, together, standing close to one another. Amar is away, one last trip before making a decision about his job. They both smile at me from a distance, looking in my direction without seeing me. I imagine a gaping hole where my body should be.

Music.

I CAN'T GET NO SATISFACTION.

Brahim and I used to dance together, spinning freely, orbiting like the sun.

His beard was soft, his abdomen hard.

I used to cling to Brahim's shoulders like a lost child seeking protection.

We found each other, we lost each other.

I don't believe in love, I believe in the memory of love.

Algeria, our starry Eldorado.

I can't get no satisfaction.

I dance alone, there's no one around me now. I go outside, I'm hot, the night sky is streaked. I climb the steps to Erwan's classroom.

I want to see my son's desk one last time, his chair, his drawings on the wall, the peg where he hung his things, the blackboard he stood in front of.

Strings of blinking lights. The moon. The town below, cargo ships preparing to leave. A clear night.

Through the classroom window, I see Catherine and Henri. She is pressed to the wall, legs spread, thighs around the Frenchman's hips.

Daylight eclipsed.

I go back down. Bruce is looking for her mother. She thinks she has a fever. She's scared, she doesn't feel well.

'She's upstairs.'

I watch from the playground as Bruce climbs the steps, walks along the hallway as far as her classroom, I watch as she opens the door and steps into the classroom.